The REAL Top Gun

A novel adaptation of the war years of
Spitfire Ace 'Johnnie' Johnson

To Carolyn

The REAL Top Gun

A novel adaptation of the war years of Spitfire Ace
'Johnnie' Johnson

by
Graham Wilding

WILDING
press limited

First published in Great Britain by
Wilding Press Limited 2013

For more information please visit
www.wildingpress.org

© 2013 Wilding Press Ltd
The REAL Top Gun (screenplay) © Wilding Press Ltd

ISBN 978-0-9927713-0-0

Cover and interior design by Vivian @ Bookscribe

Printed and bound in Great Britain by
Ashford Colour Press Ltd

CONTENTS

Preface 6

PART 1: APPRENTICESHIP 7

Chapter 1: Growing pains.................................... 8
Chapter 2: Back door 20
Chapter 3: Found out 30
Chapter 4: Bader.. 41
Chapter 5: What now?..................................... 49
Chapter 6: Welbeck Abbey................................. 56
Chapter 7: Butcher Bird.................................... 64
Chapter 8: Ace of Clubs.................................... 74
Chapter 9: Paula 81
Chapter 10: Party Town 89
Chapter 11: Canadians 95

PART 2: LEADERSHIP 101

Chapter 12: Tactics... 102
Chapter 13: Breakthrough 111
Chapter 14: Burn out....................................... 118
Chapter 15: Near miss 128
Chapter 16: Poisoned words 133
Chapter 17: The unknown 138
Chapter 18: Overlord....................................... 145
Chapter 19: Weapons of mass destruction 152
Chapter 20: Dante's Inferno................................ 160
Chapter 21: Pay day.. 168
Chapter 22: Rude awakening................................ 176
Chapter 23: Mortality 186
Chapter 24: Final crossing 192

Epilogue 200
Acknowledgements... 202
References 204

PREFACE

I first discovered the story of 'Johnnie' Johnson when I was working on a project to raise money for 'Help for Heroes'. The more I read about him, the more I realised that one of the most fascinating characters from history was being slowly forgotten. I had to ask myself, "Why is there no feature film?"

I wanted to do something to revive the memory of Johnnie in the hope that one day that film will be made. That is why I wrote this book and the screenplay of the same title.

It is often said that 'fact is stranger than fiction' and in Johnnie's case that is certainly true. During my research it became clear that my main problem was that there is simply too much to tell. His achievements were so extraordinary and so numerous that I was overwhelmed with material. The only solution I could find was to write a novel adaptation of his war years. This is not a history book or a biography, it is an interpretation.

There have been a number of excellent history books written about Johnnie and for anyone who is interested, I can recommended any of those listed in the References section on pages 204 and 205.

Graham Wilding
November 2013

PART 1
APPRENTICESHIP

Chapter One
GROWING PAINS

On a cold, grey, February afternoon in 1932, a large crowd had gathered on the playing field of Loughborough Grammar School to witness the main event in the sporting calendar – the open cross-country challenge. Boys from every year were invited to compete against one another and previous upsets had been known.

Parents, pupils and teachers were joined by local dignitaries and officers from His Majesty's Armed Forces. In front of the dignitaries the Headmaster, Mr. Pullinger, smoothed his white moustache, checked his pocket watch and slipped it back into his waistcoat pocket. Standing hunched to one side of the finishing line, Sarah was cold, bored and unimpressed. As a pretty, blonde, eighteen-year-old – who was more at home on the debutante circuit – standing on a muddy field in the depths of winter was not her idea of fun. She stamped her frozen feet and tucked her hands under her armpits.

For several weeks prior to the race there had been incessant rain in Loughborough and the roads were slippery, the fields were muddy, and the going was heavy. Only the deepest reserves of stamina and determination would crown the victor. Along Leicester Road the lead runner Armstrong, had opened a gap of some fifty yards and the outcome seemed inevitable.

To the current champion, Johnnie Johnson, winning was everything. Born in the country and a hunter since boyhood, he understood the perils of nature and the struggle for survival. In everything he did he competed as if his very life depended on it. But on this occasion he had managed to get himself boxed in tightly by a pack of runners who were falling further behind the lead. His face was splattered with mud kicked up from the runners in front, and his thick, dark hair was plastered to his forehead. He tried to elbow his way free, but each time he was elbowed back. Things were not going at all well.

When Armstrong reached the wooded section of the course, he jumped clear over a fallen log and disappeared into the darkness of the trees. A few moments later the ensuing pack scrambled over the log and one of them tripped and fell. Seizing his opportunity, Johnnie barged his way through the opened gap. In the gloom of the wood and out of sight of the spectators, Johnnie closed nimbly on his quarry. Leaves flew and twigs snapped underfoot. Armstrong looked back anxiously to see Johnnie advancing with a look of cold, predatory menace.

Once out of the wood and through the Lodge Gate, Johnnie and Armstrong turned into the view of the crowd. Packed in between the trees lining Burton Walk, the cheering spectators grew more excited as the two runners fought it out over the final two hundred yards. With leaden legs and lungs rasping for oxygen, Johnnie moved to overtake but Armstrong blocked his passage. Again and again he tried, but Armstrong would not give way. Up ahead, the turning onto the playing field could be seen and Johnnie bided his time patiently. With fifty yards to go Armstrong looked back over his right shoulder to see Johnnie within touching distance. Just as the pair turned onto the playing field, Johnnie dummied a move to the left. Armstrong moved to block again but with a neat rugby sidestep Johnnie moved to the right and out into the open space. With his view no longer obscured, Johnnie could see the finishing line. Adrenaline surged through his veins.

As they watched the thrilling neck and neck dash, the crowd reached a crescendo of fist-clenching cheers. The energy of the occasion found its way into Johnnie's legs as he pounded them for all he was worth. He dug deep, and in one last lung-bursting effort, he edged away from Armstrong and crossed the line as champion once more.

Just a couple of yards in front of Sarah, Johnnie came to a standstill, bent over with his hands on his knees and gasped for air. His rib cage heaved and then shuddered as he coughed and wiped his nose. With a satisfying feeling of achievement he straightened up, clasped his hands behind the back of his head and looked up to the sky as if to give thanks. Soaked from head to toe and with his shirt clinging around the definition of his torso, steam rose from his back and condensed breath billowed from his nose and mouth. Drawn by raw animal instinct, Sarah gazed in silence.

Once the runners-up had received their medals, the rest of the competitors formed two lines of honour in front of the crowd. Johnnie waited and faced Mr. Pullinger who stood on the podium at the opposite end of the tunnel. As he announced the winner he glanced proudly around the crowd.

"And so for the third year running, the champion of the Loughborough Grammar School Open Cross Country Challenge is – James Johnson!"

The crowd applauded as Johnnie strode between the lines of runners. Mr. Pullinger congratulated him warmly and handed over the cup. Unable to suppress his irrepressible grin, Johnnie turned and raised it in triumph. Sarah was smitten.

By the time he had reached his final year at Loughborough Grammar School Johnnie had established himself as an outstanding all-round student. He was academically bright, strong in sport and blessed with self-effacing charm and wit. Mr. Pullinger had high hopes for his star pupil and had already prepared an impressive school reference in readiness for Johnnie's application to become an RAF Officer. And now that the most eligible girl at St. Catherine's sought his affections, it seemed that there was nothing to stand in his way.

In early June, Johnnie sat cross legged on his bed and read a letter from his Uncle Charlie. During the First World War Uncle Charlie had saved himself and two of his mates from a German grenade attack. It had cost him a finger and caused paralysis in his hand, but the action had earned him the Military Cross and the post of manager of his commanding officer's rubber plantation in Malaya. The news of Johnnie's run of success was a dream come true for him, and he had penned his letter of congratulation by return of post.

As a childless bachelor, Uncle Charlie doted on Johnnie and his brother Ross as if they were his own sons, and had even paid for Johnnie's school fees. During his visits to Britain he had thrilled the two boys with his larger than life 'Boy's Own' stories. To Johnnie he was a role model beyond compare. Few things meant more to him than to make his Uncle Charlie proud.

When he had finished reading the letter, Johnnie went over to his chest of drawers on top of which was a busy collection of school and sports memorabilia. On the wall above the drawers were various pictures of military aircraft and a drawing of a futuristic German 'bat-winged' glider. He tucked the letter in the rack containing the rest of Uncle Charlie's correspondence and set off for the first of his university entrance exams.

Despite the drudgery of summer revision and cramming, Johnnie would still break away and meet Sarah whenever he could. During one still and humid early evening she waited for him by the changing cubicles of Loughborough School's open air swimming pool. Johnnie had been held up by unexpected prefect duties and was half an hour late. Fearing she might have given up and gone home, when he finally found her she was even more flushed with desire. Without saying a word she pressed herself against him through her thin cotton dress and as they kissed they stumbled backwards together through the swing door of a changing cubicle. Sarah started undressing him hastily.

"Let's get in the pool," said Johnnie.

"You're joking! Someone might see us!"

From over the top of the cubicle door they both peered around the empty pool. The evening sun sparkled invitingly on the water. Sarah looked back impishly at Johnnie.

"Go on then! I dare you!"

Without hesitation Johnnie whipped off his underpants and stood proudly with his hands on his hips.

"Oh my God!" shrieked Sarah.

"Your turn!" said Johnnie.

Sarah stripped with slow, sublime confidence. Just about every boy in Loughborough Grammar's Sixth Form fancied her, but nobody could even get close. Yet right there in front of Johnnie's eyes she stood in naked perfection. Toned and firm, her lissom curves and flawless milky white skin were as smooth as alabaster. She took the grips out of her hair, shook it loose and looked at Johnnie with impatient, arrogant desire.

Johnnie moved to kiss her, but this time Sarah snatched his clothes mischievously and ran onto the poolside. Johnnie gave chase and as he grabbed her they both tumbled into the water. In light blue silence, rays of sunlight reflected on Sarah's blurred lithe limbs and Johnnie's clothes swirled around her as she kicked for the surface. Johnnie bobbed up first and when Sarah emerged he moved towards her. Taking in a gulp of air she pushed him away and surface dived in front of him. As she approached him Johnnie looked down and watched in disbelief. After a few seconds Sarah popped up, smiled and squirted a mouthful of water in his face. With a devilish grin he lunged for her but again she evaded him and swam away. Her teasing had become too much. Johnnie swam and cornered her.

Sarah turned and faced him, calm and deliberate. No more joking. Rat-tails of her long, fair hair draped around her slender shoulders. Her blue eyes followed his every move and her lips parted. She wrapped her arms around his neck and planted her mouth on his. He dipped in the water to lift her legs round him. Her silky firm thighs gripped his waist as she crossed her ankles behind his backside. Johnnie closed his eyes.

Within a few seconds Johnnie was disturbed by a deep

anxiety, as if an uncomfortable sixth sense was telling him he was being watched. He opened his eyes to see a pair of feet in deck shoes just inches from his face. He jerked his head up to see Mr. Bradley, the Sports Master, standing over him. Behind Mr. Bradley, in the windows of the gymnasium next door, several boys had climbed up the wall bars and were laughing through the glass.

"Out! The pair of you!" barked Mr. Bradley.

Another class of boys burst out onto the poolside and the teacher's voice reverberated around the water's edge.

"Wait outside, all of you!"

The boys sniggered as they started to leave. Sarah climbed up the pool steps, glanced indignantly at the sports master and then, without bothering to cover herself, flounced back to the changing cubicles. Johnnie hurriedly collected his clothes from the water and followed her.

"Where do you think you're going Johnson?" he boomed.

As Johnnie turned he covered himself awkwardly. From the other side of the poolside door the class of boys peeped through the crack and sniggered.

"The Headmaster's study! Now!"

In dripping wet clothes Johnnie stood in front of Mr. Pullinger's desk. Behind the headmaster, the bright evening sun shone through the leaded glass window and shrouded him into a faceless, dark silhouette. He listened in silence as Mr. Bradley recalled the incident. Hearing the tail as described by another person, Johnnie thought he should feel shame and embarrassment – but strangely he didn't. Over the years he had taken several beatings at the hands of Mr. Pullinger and so he was no stranger to his study. But this time he had no fear, only feelings of intrusion. What was it to do with anyone else? Perhaps the swimming pool was a bit of a mistake, he should have taken her somewhere else, but in the heat of the moment passion had got the better of him. And – he was eighteen – he was no longer a boy. His personal life was not a matter for authority.

When Mr. Bradley had finished, Mr. Pullinger stroked his moustache and spoke with calm severity.

"Is this true, Johnson?"

"Yes, sir."

"And what do you have to say for yourself?"

"Well er, I erm. Well – it was very nice!"

"This is no laughing matter!" Mr. Pullinger bellowed with red-faced fury. "You know Sarah's family carries a title! She's supposed to be going to Oxford in October; God only knows what her father will do if this gets out."

Johnnie was cut down in an instant. "What I mean, sir, is that I am sorry. Really I am. But – well, does anyone else have to know?"

What had started out as a bit of fun was unravelling rapidly. On 'becoming a man' he had seriously underestimated the influence of his school and Mr. Pullinger's absolute power.

"Do you really think we can keep something like this quiet, Johnson? Tomorrow morning I'll have the headmistress of St. Catherine's on the phone. One of her girls has been caught naked on the school grounds and she'll want to know what I'm going to do about it."

Mr. Pullinger stood up, walked over to his study window

and surveyed the long drive, courtyard and ancient school buildings. Without turning he spoke with painful disappointment.

"You had so much going for you. You could have had it all. An officer in the armed forces; an ambassador for your school; a scholar; an athlete; someone for the younger boys to look up to."

Torn and exasperated he turned to face Johnnie and continued with vexation. "What you have done has put me – has put this school – in an impossible position."

He sat down again and faced Johnnie with an icy stare.

"I should expel you. But if I do that then the parents, the clergy, everyone would find out. But if you were to *leave*, no one would be any the wiser."

Johnnie knew Mr. Pullinger well. His own achievements were due in part to the headmaster himself who had nurtured and mentored him. He was a fair man and Johnnie knew his words could not have come easily.

"Then, sir, I think I should leave."

Mr. Pullinger was suddenly brisk and businesslike.

"Very well. You can come back to finish your exams, but after that we don't want to see you here again. There will be no record of this and what you tell your Uncle Charlie is up to you. Now go and see the Bursar."

"Yes, sir."

The decision had been made, but as Johnnie turned to leave Mr. Pullinger added one last condition.

"And, Johnson – don't ask for a reference!"

Later that same day the school caretaker removed the gold

leaf letters of J. E. Johnson from the oak wood 'Old Boy's' wall board in the school hall. In the courtyard, Johnnie walked along the drive accompanied by the porter who pushed a hand trolley loaded with his packing cases and trunks. Faces appeared at windows and boys stood in silence as if witnessing a funeral. Only the sound of footsteps and the rumble of the trolley wheels on the gravel could be heard.

At the bus stop outside the school gates the porter dropped Johnnie's belongings and then, without saying a word, turned and rumbled his way back along the drive.

Later that June, Johnnie left the examination hall of his old school for the last time. Excluded from any celebrations, he walked the short distance to the Lodge Gate and waited for Sarah as arranged. She was never late and this time he was ten minutes early. Half an hour passed and there was no sign of her. Perhaps she had got the time wrong. But after an hour it was clear she was not going to turn up. Sarah's exams did not finish for another week. Perhaps she had had some extra revision to do?

The following day Johnnie caught the bus from Melton Mowbray to Loughborough. Half an hour before the afternoon exams were due to finish he waited by the school gates of St. Catherine's. Drivers stood by rows of expensive cars which lined the drive outside. When the exam hall doors opened, Johnnie spotted Sarah walking out with a group of friends. One of them carried her exam question paper and the others crowded around to look over her shoulder. Some looked worried, some did not. Johnnie walked towards the gate but before he could go any further he was confronted by a large, upright driver.

"Stay away!" was all he said.

From a distance Johnnie stood and watched as Sarah walked over to a big Bentley. The driver opened the car door and Johnnie stepped forward into clearer view. Sarah paused to look back at him for a moment, then climbed into the back of the car and the driver closed the door.

Every morning Johnnie checked the post in the hope of receiving a letter from her. His father was a police sergeant and so the Johnson's had a telephone at their home in Welby Lane. Perhaps she would call? But as the weeks passed he began to realise that there would be no going back. Sarah had been his first; he would never see her again.

Out on the scrub of his Leicestershire homeland, Johnnie spent the rest of the summer indulging in his favourite pastime, shooting. He would often roam with his brother Ross and his black Labrador dog in search of rabbits. But it was more than just a hobby. He had bought his double barrelled shot gun on HP and had worked out that if he killed two rabbits for every three cartridges used and sold each rabbit for a shilling a piece, he would be able to pay for his gun before the autumn. Once paid up, anything after that was pocket money. As he could not afford to miss, he soon learned to be sure of the kill before pulling the trigger. Pigeons were more challenging. They would sometimes twist and turn unpredictably forcing Johnnie to anticipate their flight. As a result his marksmanship became honed and seldom would he only wound his prey.

The days passed slowly and in time the gravity of the swimming pool saga no longer seemed to matter. Eventually the letter confirming that Johnnie had passed his university entrance exams arrived. All the cramming and revision had paid off and he had secured his place at Nottingham University. Eventually the day he had been waiting for arrived, and when he returned home after an early morning shoot he found a letter waiting for him in the hall. It was from the 'Air Ministry'. His mother and father looked on expectantly as he opened it but after a few anxious moments the message was clear – 'rejected'.

That afternoon Johnnie and his mother and father, Alfred, sat around the kitchen table with the letter in front of them. Without a school reference the Auxiliary RAF would never contemplate any candidate, let alone anyone who had been asked to leave. His swimming pool tryst had cost him dearly. There was no surprise, only disappointment. But still his father Alfred, stood by him.

"Look son, what you did was a very stupid thing. But that's all it was – stupid. It could be worse, she could be pregnant."

"But what about Uncle Charlie? What will he think? He'll be devastated when he finds out."

"Your Uncle Charlie was no angel when he was your age!" said Johnnie's mother.

"But that's not the point. This was all he ever wanted for me."

"Well then, if that's the way you feel," said Alfred, "you're going to have to work out how to put this right, aren't you?"

"How? I've wrecked everything! How can I put all this right?"

"Only you can answer that."

Chapter Two
BACK DOOR

The following October Johnnie left home for Nottingham University and all the freedom that student life had to offer. Although there was as much sport, drinking and cavorting as he could manage, Johnnie never had a serious girlfriend. Flying was his one and only love and with such a long family military history, the RAF was the only way for him to achieve his dream. But no matter how he thought about it, it all came back down to the same old problem. No school reference.

But what if he could show the RAF something of greater worth? A Bachelor of Science in Civil Engineering would not be a bad start. And what if he learned to fly? When all was said and done that was what the RAF was all about. It was worth a try.

So he settled down to his studies in earnest and during college sabbaticals he went shooting on the scrubs. He sold the rabbits and pigeons he killed to the local butcher in Melton Mowbray, and with the money he made he paid for the occasional flying lesson. Shortly before he was due to graduate he resubmitted his RAF application and after a couple of weeks he was offered another chance.

During the RAF aircrew selection process most candidates failed on the medical examination and by the third day the original number of applicants was down from forty to just five. Johnnie was on the home straight, but he knew he faced an even more stringent test. On his way to the office block for his final interview Johnnie noticed a beautiful SS 90 open top sports car. Although he was a member of Melton Mowbray Car Club he could never afford a car of his own, and he spent a few minutes admiring the Jaguar's sleek lines.

RAF officer pilots generally regarded themselves as being a cut above the rest of society, and the selection process tended to be very exclusive. Families of wealthy land owners were often related or well known to interviewing officers, and successful applicants were 'traditionally' drawn from the public schools of the hunting classes.

In his interview, Johnnie faced Wing Commander Howard Davidson and Squadron Leader Gerald Stevens. Davidson was a 'traditionalist' and wore monogrammed shirts and expensive hair oil. But although both he and Stevens wore the distinctive gold 'A' lapel badges of the Auxiliary RAF, Stevens was a subliminal 'moderniser'.

Davidson had no time for any applicants whom he considered to be sub-standard and revelled in demonstrating his no-nonsense authority to his old friend. With his elbow on his desk he propped up his temple with his forefinger and thumbed casually through Johnnie's application. Then he noticed his home address and enquired as to which fox hunting pack he followed.

"Well I don't hunt with hounds, sir," said Johnnie, "I shoot."

Unimpressed, Davidson slouched back in his chair and, with an exasperated sigh, examined his fingernails until Stevens broke the awkward silence.

"I notice you're taking flying lessons, Johnson?" he remarked enthusiastically.

The flying lessons! When they realised just how many hours of shooting it took to pay for just one lesson they could not fail to be impressed. The flying was bound to clinch it.

"Yes, sir." Said Johnnie, "I pay for them by selling the rabbits and pigeons I shoot, to the local butcher and . . ."

"Yes, you've already mentioned that!" interrupted Davidson impatiently. "Where's your school reference?"

Johnnie's hunch was dismissed in an instant as Davidson homed in on its conspicuous absence.

"I don't have one, sir," Johnnie admitted, "I left too soon."

"What do you mean? 'Don't have one!' Everyone has a school reference!"

Finally, Davidson closed Johnnie's file.

"And now you're studying to become a Civil Engineer. At least Nottingham has confirmed that. Perhaps you should go and build air raid shelters or something."

And that was that. Johnnie politely thanked the two officers and left. Later, Davidson sifted through the pile of applications, taking cursory glances at the top pages.

"Just look at this lot!" he grumbled, "I mean, I've never even heard of some of these schools. How on earth are we supposed to have any idea of what these lads are like?"

"I thought Johnson was quite interesting," said Stevens.

"School, Gerald, School! If a headmaster is not prepared to give a chap a reference then he has no place in the RAF."

"He can still fly an aeroplane!"

"You have to be able to ride a horse to *really* fly an aeroplane.

That Johnson comes from one of the greatest fox hunting areas of Britain and he goes hunting with a gun! I ask you?"

In 1935 Johnnie finally graduated with a degree in Civil Engineering and it was time to look for his first job. In Germany, Hitler had been in power for two years and Nazi rearmament was causing international concern. There was even talk of another war. Locally, Johnnie's father had to deal with skirmishes stoked up by some of the members of the local fascist party.

On a warm afternoon in late August, Johnnie and Ross were out shooting on the scrub. Ross was laden with dead rabbits and the two brothers were about to leave for the butcher's shop when a couple of fast, low-flying pigeons came into range. Johnnie quickly loaded and as they raced across his sights he took each one down with a single shot. He got paid less for pigeon but that didn't matter. It took a keen eye and cat-like reflexes to make clean kills of two birds on the turn.

By the time Johnnie and Ross arrived back at the square in Melton Mowbray it was late afternoon, and a large crowd had gathered to listen to the leader of the local branch of the British Fascist Party speak. Large banners were unfurled, intimidating henchmen in white shirts and black ties stood at strategic points. A van with two large loudspeakers on the roof was parked next to the makeshift wooden stage from where Less Till addressed the crowd. Johnnie and Ross passed by the crowd and into the butcher's shop. Inside the shop the butcher slapped seven shillings and sixpence onto the marble counter top. Johnnie collected his earnings and paid Ross sixpence. When they came out again the mood of the crowd was becoming heated as Less Till yelled into the microphone.

"I come to you with a new virile faith of fascism ..."

From across the other side of the square Johnnie and Ross saw their father approaching the crowd.

"... Lift up your voices and tell the whole world that England lives and marches on!" Till ranted.

As Alfred pushed his way through the crowd and up to the stage, Till watched his approach nervously.

"Uncle Alfred!" he said feebly.

"Sergeant Johnson to you, laddie!"

A group of henchmen stepped forward and surrounded Alfred, who merely glanced at them with dismissive contempt.

"You tell these men they've got five minutes to break this lot up."

In the tense, precipitous pause, the largest of the henchmen closed in, but there was no response from Alfred, just the cold predatory Johnson stare. Humiliated, Till nodded and signalled to his henchman to leave. The crowd began to disperse and the square slowly began to return to normal. Johnnie's father had won the moment but the message was uncomfortably clear – war was on its way!

As Alfred Johnson walked home with his two sons, Johnnie had some news for him.

"I've got that surveyor's job in Lancashire, Father."

"Which one's that?"

"The one in the Town Hall in Poulton le Fylde. It's near Blackpool and so it means I can carry on flying. And I've heard the RAF might be forming a reservist group which means *anyone* can apply!"

The small market town of Poulton le Fylde was similar in many ways to Melton Mowbray and Johnnie managed to keep his eye in with rabbit shooting by courtesy of the local farmers. The flying from Squire's Gate airport was good too and, with Blackpool Tower nearby, no one could get lost. But the job was only temporary and the next post took Johnnie to the mining town of Staveley in Derbyshire.

Many of the coal mines and cottages in that area were owned by the Duke of Portland and while in his employment, Johnnie was sent to inspect them.

On his first morning in November 1935, Johnnie walked with his briefcase along one of the town's many back alleys. Above the slate rooftops of the terraced houses, a winding tower jutted up in front of the grey spoil tips. Washing hung across the way, girls played hopscotch and boys played football with a tin can. Dogs barked and children shrieked. A wagon pulled up next to a row of outside toilets. Soil men climbed out of its cab and took large metal tubs from under each toilet and emptied them into the back of the wagon. Sewage, pieces of newspaper and cinders slopped out in a mixture of slurry and dust. As he walked past the wagon on the way to his first call, Johnnie choked on the stench. For a country boy who was used to the open fields of Leicestershire, life in Staveley was to be a whole new education.

With the increasing threat of war, the following year the RAF Volunteer Reserve came into being and Johnnie wasted no time in submitting his application. At the busy Aircrew Selection

Centre at Store Street, London, a great many applicants were processed through the various stages. Regarded by some in the Auxiliary as the 'back door', the Volunteer Reserve invited men from all kinds of occupations to try their luck. Barristers, farm labourers, bank clerks and car mechanics, they all wanted to fly and fight.

During his interview, Johnnie's lack of school reference drew little more than a few raised eyebrows, but still the outcome was the same and the interviewing officer sounded almost apologetic.

"You see a real shooting war has not actually started yet," he said, "and so we're not recruiting at the moment. I'm sorry – Government policy! But we'll keep your application on record and if anything changes we'll be in touch."

Flight training for most Volunteer Reservists was based at airfields in the South of England. Mid-week nightschools were also held at Store Street and all trainee reservists were expected to attend. It was clear that a move to the south of England would be essential and eventually Johnnie found a new job at Loughton near Epping Forrest.

Shortly after his arrival there, he joined Chingford Rugby Club and it was during a match on one freezing cold day that his flying career was almost ended before it had started. Chingford were playing against Park House and Johnnie was on the wing. Spectators in heavy overcoats and scarves shouted their encouragement from an old double-decker bus which was used as a makeshift stand. With the scores level, the game was keenly contested. Late in the second half Johnnie spotted a gap in the opposition defence and made a break with the ball. But just a few yards from the line he was tackled hard and brought down onto the frozen grass. With a sickeningly audible crack he felt a sharp stab of pain in his right shoulder.

The referee stopped the match and Johnnie rose to his feet cupping his right elbow in his left hand.

"You alright?" asked the referee.

Johnnie gave a painful nod.

"Let me see."

The referee pulled the neck of Johnnie's shirt to one side and looked at his shoulder.

"That looks broken to me. Off you go."

As Johnnie walked towards the touchline the players and spectators applauded. The captain made his substitution and the referee restarted the match.

In the casualty department of the local hospital the duty doctor confirmed a complicated fracture of Johnnie's collar bone. But, despite having lost all sensation in his right hand, the doctor also told him there was nothing further that could be done.

"What about flying?" asked Johnnie.

The doctor flicked the X-ray film down off the viewer and regarded him imperiously over the rim of his spectacles.

"What about it?"

"I want to be a pilot. Is this thing going to stop me?"

The doctor slipped the X-ray film into a large brown envelope.

"Look, there are thousands of young men out there, all just like you. And they all want to be pilots."

"I know," said Johnnie, "but is this thing going to stop me from flying?"

"That's a matter for the aviation medics I'm afraid. But no more rugby for you this season."

Several months later, Johnnie returned from work to his flat to find a letter from the Air Ministry waiting for him on his door mat. The interviewing officer had been true to his word and had written to him inviting him to attend a further interview at Store Street.

Once again Johnnie went through the usual tests – medical, eyesight, aptitude, coordination, reflexes, aircraft recognition and academic papers. But before the final interview the medical officer wanted to see him again. Stripped to the waist, he was quizzed once more.

"Rugby injury, you say – ever given you any trouble?"

"No, not a bit," Johnnie lied.

The doctor prodded Johnnie's injured shoulder hard but he did not notice him flinch. Then he pinched Johnnie's right hand hard and looked him straight in the face.

"Feel that?"

"Ow! Yes," said Johnnie, not feeling a thing.

"Right then, arms in the air, now out to the side, and down again. Any problem?"

"No."

The Medical Officer went back to his desk and stamped Johnnie's medical form 'A1'.

At the end of the selection process the remaining candidates were gathered into a sparse, highly polished briefing room. Of the eight men, Johnnie had already got to know two of them. Roy was from Manchester and Nick was from Newcastle upon Tyne. Both shared Johnnie's wry sense of humour and the three men sat together. Previous selections had always followed the same pattern but they had never concluded with a gathering such as this one. Johnnie turned to Nick.

"What do you think all this is about?"

"Divant knah, man!" answered the Geordie.

The door opened and a very confident Flight Lieutenant walked into the room, closed it behind him and stood in front of the men. Not knowing quite what to do they all stood up.

"That's alright, you can sit down," said the Flight Lieutenant. "You have all been selected for aircrew. Once you have been sworn in you will commence training as Sergeant Pilots for the duration of hostilities."

He was in!

Chapter Three
FOUND OUT

On 1 September 1939, Germany invaded Poland and Britain was plunged into another war. But it was an event which ensured that Johnnie would at last train as an RAF pilot. A few days later he put on his RAF sergeant uniform for the first time and later arrived at Cambridge railway station along with two hundred other Volunteer Reservists. They were all promptly marched into the quadrangle of Jesus College where they were allocated temporary accommodation and given details of their forthcoming curriculum.

The country was in desperate need of five thousand new pilots and over the winter months the flight training pressure on students and instructors alike was relentless. Johnnie's original flying lessons paid off and his progress was relatively uneventful. But despite his best efforts he could only manage a grade of 'average' and in war – average would not be good enough to survive. His problem was his old rugby injury. The tight cockpit harness pulled on it agonisingly and disrupted his concentration. Self doubt began to creep in.

Shortly after the outbreak of war Britain sent troops to fight alongside the French in an attempt to prevent a Nazi invasion of France. But by May 1940 it was all over and the British and French forces were forced to flee back to Britain through Dunkirk. The 'Spitfire' was the new fighter aeroplane upon which Britain's survival in an air battle depended, but when

Churchill became the new Prime Minister its rate of production was dismally slow. So one of Churchill's first decisions as head of the War Cabinet, was to put the no-nonsense Canadian, Lord Beaverbrook, in charge of its mass production. It proved to be a shrewd appointment and within weeks Beaverbrook had Spitfires rolling off the new production line at Castle Bromwich, Birmingham, at the rate of four hundred per month.

By mid-June 1940, Nazi troops marched into Paris and Churchill gave his grim assessment of the consequences over the radio:

> *"... the battle of France is over, the Battle of Britain is about to begin. The whole fury and might of the enemy must very soon be turned upon us. Hitler knows that he will have to break us in this island or lose the war..."*

The stage was set for a major air battle between the RAF and the Luftwaffe, but if Johnnie was going to be in it he first had to get onto Spitfires. At a time when there was a national shortage of the precious fighters, his flying grade was still only average.

On completion of his basic flight training he was sent to Sealand Airfield near Chester to learn how to shoot while flying an aeroplane. But when he reported to the Sergeant's Mess to receive his accommodation instructions, the office sergeant shook his head.

"There's no 'Sergeant Johnson' on my list," he said.

"Are you sure?" asked Johnnie. "My instructions are quite clear, look."

Johnnie unbuttoned his breast pocket and handed over a

folded piece of paper. The office sergeant unfolded it and read it aloud.

"J. E. Johnson?" he puzzled and walked over to the filing cabinet. After flicking through the sleeves, he pulled out a letter and handed it over to Johnnie.

"You're in the wrong place," said the sergeant.

"But this is the Sergeant's Mess, isn't it?" asked Johnnie opening the letter.

"Yes, but you're not Sergeant Pilot Johnson. You're Cadet Officer Johnson. I have it in writing, here. Congratulations, sir. I'll have someone show you to the Officer's Mess."

Promotion to officer from the ranks would normally take years of RAF service and strict scrutiny. Johnnie had done it in less than nine months. He reported to the Officer's Mess where he was told to report immediately to the Commanding Officer (CO). One of the mess servants showed him to the dormitory and after he had dumped his kit bag on his bed he set off for the CO's office.

Parked outside the CO's office he recognised the same green Jaguar SS which he had seen when he attended the interview with the Auxiliary RAF.

Wing Commander Davidson did not care much for the Volunteer Reserve, nor did he care for the 'modernisation' of the RAF, he preferred more traditional methods. "Reliable chaps from reliable backgrounds," was his mantra. When Johnnie reported to his office Davidson kept him to attention.

"I've been checking through your previous applications, Johnson. It would appear that third time really is lucky."

"Yes, sir!"

"And someone has even decided that you are officer material!"

"Thank you, sir."

"That someone was not me. I can only think that this has something to do with your degree from Nottingham. Nevertheless, once you have received your commission you are to train on Spitfires."

"Thank you, sir!"

Davidson leaned his elbows on his desk and cupped the clenched fist of one hand in the other and regarded Johnnie with thinly veiled contempt.

"There's something not right about you, Johnson. Now I don't know what it is and I'm not going to waste my time trying to find out, but just remember this – you're being watched."

In the Officer's Mess dormitory some of the more seasoned pilots of the Auxiliary prepared themselves for dinner. They paid little regard to Johnnie and he unpacked his belongings just as he had done as a new boy at Loughborough. But this was no schoolboy dormitory. The floor was immaculately polished, the metal lockers were clean and tidy and all the bedding was rolled up and stacked on neat rows of metal framed beds. The atmosphere was all rather more civilised too, or so it seemed. During his time at school he had seen model pupils behave impeccably in the presence of masters and prefects, only to behave like gangsters after lights-out. Weighing up the pecking order, he finished unpacking with his head down and his thoughts to himself.

He was just about to go to the dining room when he was joined by Roy and Nick, the two candidates he had met at Store Street and immediately Johnnie no longer felt like the 'new boy'. After a quick bit of unpacking and an exchange of first impressions, the three of them left the dormitory for dinner.

Unlike the usual clatter of the sparse Sergeant's canteen, the Officer's Mess lounge could not have been more different. The carpets and armchairs would have looked more in place in a smart hotel, the bar was well stocked and the officers were served by smart, middle-aged men in short, white coats. Uncertain at first, the three newcomers paused in the doorway.

Auxiliary pilots completely dominated the room. Some wore their ties bulging ostentatiously while others left their jackets open displaying their exclusive crimson silk linings. Their laughter was more of a series of loud cultivated guffaws and they breezed to and from the bar with absolute self assurance.

"I'd like to see them ponse around like that in Salford," said Roy.

Johnnie was the first to open up his mess bill and once they were half way down their first pints they moved among the rest of the pilots in the hope of getting to know some of them. Straining their ears, they tried to glean some sense from the hubbub of the room. But the drifting jargon of 'line abreast' and 'tail end Charlie' meant nothing to them. Trying to join in conversation was useless. With their backs turned and in tight little cliques, the Auxiliary was strictly for members only.

During training there was no let up in the pressure cooker of pilot production and the training was intense. Flying every day from first thing in the morning and cramming at night, within weeks of arriving at Sealand Johnnie had earned his wings and a full officer's commission. With the Pilot Officer Stripe on his sleeve and the distinctive wings above his breast pocket, at least his uniform looked more the part even if he was still ignored in the bar.

But as the speed of his flying and the exertion of aerobatics became more demanding, the cockpit harness pulled harder on Johnnie's old rugby injury and sometimes the pain would prevent him from using his right hand. Knowing that he would never progress with one-handed flying, he started packing a thick pad of cotton wool under his tunic to protect his broken collar bone. His shoulder still pained him but the padding was just enough to get him through each flight and he managed to keep the secret to himself.

Just prior to the Nazi invasion of Poland, the Polish Air Force had been almost completely destroyed on the ground by the Luftwaffe. The RAF High Command was determined that such a fate should not befall their own fighter squadrons and so they were scattered around Britain in a large number of small satellite bases away from the main airfields. One such airfield was Hawarden, which was near Sealand, and it was there that Johnnie had his first flying encounter with a Spitfire.

The day he walked out onto the airfield with Flight Lieutenant Walters, his Spitfire instructor, was a day he would never forget. When he got close up to the aeroplane which was Britain's last hope, it seemed smaller than he had imagined. Walters took him on a guided tour and casually pointed out the various flight controls. There he was within touching distance of the most beautiful aircraft in the world – and by the end of the day he would be flying it. It was almost too much to believe and it was all he could do to listen as Walters rattled off endless check lists. All Johnnie wanted to do was to take her up and let the love affair begin.

At last he was allowed to climb into the cockpit and, crouching on the wing root, Walters helped him adjust the seat harness.

"No!" he said, "it needs to be much tighter over the shoulder or in battle you'll get thrown all over the place. Here like this."

Walters pulled the harness tight and Johnnie jolted as an agonising bayonet of pain stabbed in his shoulder and all the way down his arm.

"Are you alright?" asked Walters.

"Yes, yes – fine," Johnnie gasped, "the cockpit's just a little narrow across the shoulder that's all."

"You'll get use to it. You'll wish you were smaller when you get one of those yellow-nosed bastards on your arse! Now, start her up."

MAGNETOS ON
FUEL STOP COCK OPEN
THROTTLE SET
GENERATOR ON
START

The starter whirred, the propeller turned slowly and then flicked into a blur as the huge Rolls Royce Merlin engine roared into life. The whole Spitfire shuddered, sending vibrations through every muscle and bone of Johnnie's body. His shoulder hurt like hell but he was too excited to care. He had always imagined being filled with apprehension, but sitting in that tiny cockpit and cradled by those smooth elliptical wings was somehow friendly and reassuring. Walters jumped down from the wing, ambled away a few yards and signalled him for take-off.

As he taxied across the airfield, Johnnie repeatedly yawed the high nose of the Spitfire to the left and right to check for clearance ahead. Then opening up the throttle he rumbled along the grass until, surprisingly quickly, the noise stopped. Airborne! He retracted the wheels, slid the canopy shut and for the first time he felt the true confinement of the cockpit.

At first the speed and power was intimidating but as he began to feel the Spitfire's obedient response, Johnnie's confidence grew. After he had reached two hundred miles per hour he overtook one of his old training aircraft and decided it was time for a few manoeuvres. Left turn, right turn, steep climb, level out and finally into a barrel roll.

All too soon it was time to return to Hawarden. He set himself up on the approach just as had been taught in ground school. The airfield came into view but the constant pressure from the harness on his shoulder became unbearable. No longer able to control the joystick with his right hand, he swapped to his left and lost control of the throttle.

UNDERCARRIAGE: DOWN
AIRSPEED: 140 MPH
FLAPS: DOWN
HEIGHT: 250 FT

Everything was lined up correctly. Gently down. Sinking, sinking . . .

Too Fast! The Spitfire fell, hit the ground with a hefty smack and reared up again. As he watched Johnnie bounce all the way along the grass in a series of hard undignified Kangaroo hops, Walters closed his eyes and shook his head.

Four days later:
Gerald Stevens had just arrived at Hawarden to celebrate his recent promotion and he was standing with Davidson. From the edge of the landing strip the two Wing commanders watched Johnnie's approach. At fifty feet the engine stuttered and he dropped like a stone. When he hit the ground one wheel of the Spitfire was torn off and the other one was punched up through the wing. Half on its belly it slewed across the grass, spun in a half turn and finally came to a halt.

Johnnie was thrown hard into the harness which wrenched excruciatingly at his shoulder. Facing the way he had landed he looked through the smoke to see the long, deep furrow he had just ploughed in the field. Emergency bells rang behind him as a fire engine and ambulance raced towards him. He slumped back in his seat and flicked off the master switch and nursed his shoulder as the gyro compass whined and slowed down. Stevens and Davidson looked on as the ambulance crew helped Johnnie from his cockpit but when they helped him with his shoulder he simply shook his head and walked away.

The RAF could not afford to waste time on failure and if Johnnie didn't start getting it right he knew he would be out. Although his shoulder was making flying impossible, he remembered how many candidates at Store Street were failed on their medical exams. If he reported his injury there was every chance that the Medical Officer might fail him too. All he could do was keep quiet and press on to the next stage of his training.

Airborne target practice involved a lead aircraft towing a dummy aircraft or 'drogue' which student pilots would fly up to try and hit. During ground school, gunnery instructors drew all kinds of elaborate diagrams to illustrate how to shoot at aeroplanes that were twisting and turning. The diagrams were backed up with complicated mathematical formulae which students were expected to work out mentally in the few seconds they had before pressing the firing button. Some claimed that they could make sense of it all but only a few ever managed to hit anything.

As far as Johnnie was concerned the swerving and weaving drogues behaved no differently to pigeons and he had never used diagrams and maths to hit them. He simply lined himself up, just as he always had out on the fields at home and when the shot felt right – he took it. He passed swiftly through the course with an almost perfect score.

However, the problem of his shoulder still bedevilled his flying, and his landings were notoriously poor. Comments were made and despite his marksmanship he was on the brink of being taken off flight training for good. Inevitably he was confronted by Walters and fearing that he was about to be written off, he finally admitted everything. Following a couple of sessions with the Medical Officer a full report was filed and Johnnie was ordered to report to Davidson.

Yet again in Davidson's office Johnnie was kept to attention as the Wing Commander read his medical report. Next to the report on Davidson's desk lay a red ink pad and a rubber stamp bearing the letters 'LMF' (Lack of Moral Fibre).

"I had my doubts about you from the start, Johnson." As he spoke Davidson twirled the stamp between his fingers and then inked it. "You've wrecked two Spits, your landings are appalling and now the Doc tells me that you have an 'affliction' to your shoulder."

He looked out of the window.

"I don't need to tell you that the country is short of Spitfires!"

"No, sir," answered Johnnie respectfully.

"Fortunately for you, the country is also short of pilots. The Docs also tell me that you could have your shoulder corrected by surgery. So you could take your chance in hospital or I could send you to train new recruits. It's up to you."

"When can I have the operation, sir?" asked Johnnie with huge relief.

"Straight away, but it means you'll be off flying for months."

"Thank you, sir."

"Don't thank me, thank the war!"

Chapter Four
BADER

On the 20 September 1940, as the Battle of Britain was being fought in the skies over southern England, Johnnie underwent surgery on his collar bone at the RAF hospital at Rauceby, Lincolnshire. By the end of October the Luftwaffe had given up and Britain was safe from invasion – for the time being. The surgery on Johnnie's shoulder was a success but the recovery was long and painful and he had to wait until December before being returned to active service.

Just before Christmas he was posted to RAF Tangmere in West Sussex and when he arrived he found Roy and Nick in the Officer's Mess bar. But it was something of a surprise to find that they had a most unlikely new friend in Hugh, a member of the elitist Auxiliary RAF. At six foot six, skinny and with blond, curly hair and fine, sharp features, Hugh looked like he could barely fit into a Spitfire let alone have the strength to fly one.

Johnnie was suspicious at first, but after a few beers and some reassurance from Roy, the four men started to get along. Despite his somewhat aristocratic demeanour, Hugh was in fact quite a tough character. Although in the air he was not the best of shots, he was a very able pilot and a tenacious fighter. Like Johnnie he had just returned to flying duties after recovering from injury.

"Shot up on a Rhubarb over France," said Hugh, "only just made it back to Blighty."

"What's a Rhubarb?" asked Johnnie..

"You'll find out soon enough. Bloody silly if you ask me!"

In comparison to the frantic days of the previous summer of fighting, winter was quiet. Johnnie managed to get on the occasional mission to hunt enemy bombers and claimed his first 'half kill' against a Dornier, but there was little in the way of combat against enemy fighters. It seemed everything he had worked and trained for was coming to nothing and like the rest of the pilots at Tangmere he grew bored and restless. After New Year had passed uneventfully, everyone hoped the spring would see a return to what they had been trained to fight.

In early March 1941, the station began to buzz with a rumour that a new Wing Commander by the name of Douglas Bader was on his way. Following a flying accident in which he lost both legs ten years previously, Bader had originally been discharged from the RAF on medical grounds and he had had to wait for the outbreak of war before being re-enlisted. During the Battle of Britain he had emerged as an ace fighter and had become a legend throughout the entire nation and beyond. When it came to combat, it was Bader who set the standard. He was the man with whom most pilots wanted to fly and he was going to be Johnnie's new leader.

Still very much a novice, when the other pilots of the squadron rested after flying duties, Johnnie would keep himself busy by getting to know every inch of the aeroplane he hoped he would soon fly in battle. Unlike many in the Auxiliary RAF he never minded getting his hands dirty on maintenance, and one morning in early April when he had climbed into the cockpit of his Spitfire, he sat on a spanner. As he bent down to move it onto the floor of the cockpit next to a copy of a Spitfire manual, he heard a most peculiar stumping noise. He looked back up to see a stocky Wing Commander approaching in a most unusual way. The officer walked by leaning forwards and flicking the knees of his artificial legs. It could only have been Bader. Johnnie hastily climbed out of the cockpit and came to attention. Bader stood next to him.

"That's alright, sit down," he said. "What's your name?"

"Johnnie Johnson, sir."

"And where's everyone else, Johnnie?

When Johnnie explained that the rest of the squadron were in bed after night flying duties, the grumpy Wing Commander realised there would be no missions that morning. He jabbed his pipe in his mouth and spoke in between lighting it with a match.

"What's your score?" asked Bader lighting his pipe with a match.

"Nil, sir," answered Johnnie somewhat sheepishly, "I've not been able to get on many combat missions."

"Why not?"

"Just bad luck, sir."

"You make your own luck in this war," insisted Bader, "and there's only one way to fight it. You have to get up there and find the buggers. Come on, let's nip across the Channel and see if we can bag a couple of Huns before lunch."

The next thing Johnnie knew he was flying over the English Channel alongside the most famous pilot in Britain. There had been no clearance from the Station Commander and no chit chat with the control tower. The pair had just climbed in their Spitfires and taken off. Unsurprisingly it did not take too long for them to be picked up on radar and a duty officer called Bader over the radio. Johnnie listened in silence to the impatient crackly conversation.

"Swallow to Dogsbody," called the duty officer, "what are your intentions?"

"Nothing much," replied Bader. "Just a little snoop over the Channel that's all."

After a couple of minutes the duty officer called again.

"Dogsbody, you are to return to base immediately, Station Commander's orders."

Irritated by having been found out, Bader called Johnnie over the radio.

"Right, Johnnie!" he said. "Imagine we've got the Hun in our sights and we're about to shoot him down. The first thing he will do is go into a fast dive – so let's follow him."

Staying with Bader, Johnnie pushed the stick forwards and opened up to full throttle. The airspeed increased rapidly and the spanner and Spitfire manual floated in weightless suspension around his face. As he moved them to one side his engine began to stutter, the propeller windmilled lazily and he slowed down.

"In a fast dive the petrol can't get to the engine and it cuts out," Bader explained, "now let's see what happens if we flick her over. Half roll right!"

Together they both rolled over and dived upside down. Almost immediately the engines restarted.

"Now we can follow him all the way down. It means we have

to take the shot inverted, but at least we can still nail him. Fire when ready . . . and . . ."

As he listened to Bader blowing loud schoolboy raspberries in mock machine gun fire, Johnnie's thumb hovered over the button.

"What would it be like?" he asked himself. "What would it really be like?"

Back at Tangmere, Johnnie waited by Bader's Spitfire as he climbed down from his cockpit. Bader had a paternal safeguard of his pilots and it was the first time Johnnie had experienced such genuine interest in his flying.

"Nothing wrong with that!" said Bader, as they walked across the airfield.

"Thank you, sir."

"You know you can make the Spit do anything you want, it's just a matter of confidence. Whose section are you in?"

"Well I haven't really got one at the moment, sir," Johnnie said hesitantly.

"Right then, that settles it! From now on you're in mine, with Hugh Dundas."

Within the space of a short, chance encounter Johnnie had gone from being a no-one to a member of one of the most coveted sections in Fighter Command. With a man like Bader looking over him, he knew it would only be a matter of time before he would get his first taste of real combat – but not before he would find out what the mysterious 'Rhubarb' missions were all about.

Notoriously dangerous and unpopular, Rhubarb missions were strictly for volunteers only. But as impatience got the better of him, when Johnnie got his first chance he did not hesitate and his Rhubarb initiation came on the morning after a long night of ferocious alcohol-fuelled 'Mess Rugby'. A vigorous and often violent version of the outdoor game, mess rugby was played in the dining room. Fuelled by formidable amounts of alcohol it would often go on until four in the morning or until the last man standing.

As two of Tangmere's most enthusiastic Mess Rugby players, Johnnie and Hugh had only managed two hours sleep before they walked across the airfield nursing vice-like hangovers. Hugh produced a small bottle of prescribed amphetamine, unscrewed the cap and dropped a couple of tablets onto the palm of his hand.

"Pick me up?" he asked.

Feeling as if he was about to be sick Johnnie politely declined and so Hugh swallowed them both.

"Basically," he explained, "we hide in the clouds over France, drop down and take a peep – and if we can find any Germans we shoot them. Told you! Bloody silly!"

As soon as Johnnie climbed into his cockpit he switched on the oxygen, put the mask over his face and sucked deep on the pure gas in an attempt to clear his head. Then with his canopy still open, he took off and followed Hugh who led him up and into the clouds over France.

Barely able to see one another, they very soon became separated. With only his compass to guide him, Johnnie decided to drop into clear sky and get his bearings. As he cleared below the cloud Hugh's wing tip swerved in front of him and he had to yank the stick hard to the right to avoid him. Almost immediately enemy defences of northern France spotted the conspicuous elliptical wings of the two Spitfires and heavy flak broke out all around them.

Wondering what he was supposed to do next, Johnnie looked around for something to shoot at. Having spotted a column of German staff cars driving along a country road Hugh waved at him and moved into attack. Johnnie followed him down but he could see from his angle that Hugh would undershoot – eight rows of machine gun rounds ripped harmlessly past the target.

Hugh pulled up out of the dive and, as Johnnie followed into the attack, he aimed a little higher. Dust kicked up on the road and then rows of orange tracer sliced from one car to the next. Two burst into flames while another one careered off the road and into a ditch. Only one managed to escape but by then they were being buffeted so hard by the flak that Johnnie and Hugh were forced to climb back up into the cover of the clouds.

After they landed at Westhampnett, a satellite airfield near the main Tangmere base, they made their way over to Shopwyke Manor for lunch. After their hectic morning of dodging flak and each other, they waited to be served on the lawn outside. With their shirts still damp with sweat and smelling strongly of aviation fuel, they reclined in basket chairs.

The French windows of the large drawing room were wide open and net curtains billowed out through them. Inside, a pilot played a movement from Beethoven on the grand piano and the sound drifted gently across the neatly manicured garden. In comparison with the nightmare of only a few minutes earlier, it was a bizarrely peaceful setting.

Two WAAF's, dressed in floral dungarees and blouses, walked out of the drawing room carrying trays of tea. One of them walked over in Johnnie and Hugh's direction, placed a tray on the table and proceeded to serve. The two men straightened up appreciatively and Johnnie caught the girl's eye with a broad grin. To Hugh's irritation, flirtatious glances were exchanged before the WAAF took the tray and made her way back into the drawing room. Hugh lit a cigarette, took a deep drag and slouched back in his chair. After a few thoughtful sips of tea Johnnie reflected on the morning's activities.

"They could have been French, you know," he said.

"Eh?"

"Those people in those cars, Hugh. They could have been French."

"Well there wasn't time to stop and ask, was there?"

"Bader's right you know – and so are you. We should be getting stuck into some proper fighting, not hiding in clouds."

Chapter Five
WHAT NOW?

With the Nazi invasion of Britain no longer a threat, the pilots of Fighter Command went in search of the Luftwaffe over in France. But it was not an easy task as the Messerschmitt pilots would only get up to fight if their airfields were being bombed. As most of the RAF's bombing raids were carried out at night, Johnnie began to wonder if he would ever get to grips with the enemy. Night fighting and Rhubarbs were all that he could hope for.

During training Bader kept them all hard at it with daily aerobatic practice, disciplined formation flying and tactics. When going into the attack, the usual procedure was for the leader to pick one enemy aircraft while his three wingmen protected him. For the wingmen, therefore, it was a chance affair of waiting to be attacked before fighting back. It was a passive form of engagement which frustrated Johnnie and he considered it to be a waste of three 'minder' pilots who should be in the fight right from the start. But then again who was he to say? He was only an apprentice.

By early August things had become so quiet at Tangmere that Bader finally ran out of patience. Late one evening in the Officers Mess he took matters into his own hands and phoned the RAF High Command. The Air Vice Marshall on the other end of the phone took the call from his bedside and Bader made his feelings known. Fully expecting a stiff reprimand for their Wing Commander, Johnnie and Hugh sat and listened in astonishment as Bader talked his way around the senior officer. It was a lesson in diplomacy, persuasion and determination which made a lasting impression.

Sure enough the following Saturday morning, 9th August, Johnnie and Hugh sat waiting in a dispersal hut at Tangmere with the rest of the squadron. Having been out of action for so long, Johnnie's stomach was tight and he felt nauseous with nerves. A car arrived outside and the sounds of the doors opening and closing were followed by the familiar stumping noises of artificial legs. The door opened and with his usual air of indefatigable confidence Bader breezed into the hut, stood in front of a large map of France and began his brief:

"It's all quite straight forward," he said. "In one hour's time we're going to escort a section of Stirling bombers in a raid on the airfield at Abbeville, here. That should stir up the Hun fighters and we can get stuck into them – and it's the weekend so they should be about ... "

Bader's quip gave rise to a tension-breaking ripple of laugher.

" ... but if they don't want to come out and play we're going to take the piss out of them ..."

More laughter followed as the atmosphere changed from self doubt to optimism.

" ... with a little aerobatic display right over their own airfield!"

Within minutes the mood inside the hut had been transformed. Gone were the nerves and optimism prevailed. They were going to win!

One hour later, three sections of four Spitfires flew out over the English Channel. As they passed over the beaches of Northern France a thick barrage of flak broke out and then faded away again as they left the coastal defences behind. They all watched in expectation as one mile in front of them the Stirlings unloaded their bombs and turned for home.

"Dogsbody to all sections," called Bader over the radio. "There are the bomber's now. Yellow section, you keep on my starboard side and blue section keep to port. Turning now."

All twelve Spitfires started a wide left turn when Hugh spotted sections of enemy fighters climbing up.

"Dogsbody," he called calmly, "Twenty Messerschmitts, three o'clock low."

"Okay, I have then," announced Bader, "Going down. All sections follow me."

As Bader chose a target his three wingmen guarded either side of him with Johnnie second to his right. Far over to the left Johnnie spotted a stray enemy fighter climbing up into the attack. He side-slipped down towards it in a counter attack and as he did so, passed beneath the oil-stained under bellies of Hugh and Bader's Spitfires. Bader opened fire and a stream of empty shells rained down from under his wings.

Unaware of Johnnie's presence the stray Messerschmitt turned across Johnnie's sights. After his first short burst missed, he adjusted the angle of his aim and pressed the firing button again. The stick shook in his hands. Cannon and machine gun rounds flew from his wings and ripped through the engine of the target. Pieces of metal flew off the damaged aircraft and black smoke streamed in front of Johnnie's cockpit as the enemy pilot bailed out.

Hugh broke in again with an urgent call.

"It's a trap! It's a trap. Forty, repeat forty 109s five o'clock high! Break! Break!"

All the Spitfires immediately broke away in all directions. Within an instant, Johnnie was all alone in the middle of an angry swarm of enemy fighters. As he turned for the safety of the clouds he checked behind and saw three 109s on his tail. Above him to his right Bader was continuing his attack with no wingman, when an enemy fighter moved into position behind him.

"On your tail, Dogsbody, on your tail!" Johnnie shouted. "Break! For God's sake break!"

He had just a couple of seconds to warn his leader before one of the 109s behind him opened up. Johnnie rolled over into an inverted dive as orange tracer flashed past his wings. He pushed the throttle to full and the engine screamed. The altimeter spun down rapidly. At over 400 mph the needle of the air speed indicator turned into the red and he shot into the clouds.

The 109s broke off their attack. Inside the cloud Johnnie cut the throttle and the engine quietened. But the instruments flickered wildly and he became hopelessly disorientated in the swirling, white mist. The cloud hissed and he felt himself being thrown around as if on a fairground ride. On and on, round and around the altimeter continued winding down and eventually he dropped out into clear sky.

Suddenly he was in bright sunshine again and beneath him the ground whirled as his Spitfire spiralled in a flat spin.

Johnnie kicked the rudder hard against it, the spinning stopped and the nose fell forwards into a vertical dive. As he eased the stick he increased the throttle gently and levelled out.

Checking all around to get his bearings, Johnnie spotted what looked like one of the three fighters which had just attacked him. Perhaps the pilot had anticipated Johnnie's exit and had flown around to greet him. But in the deadly game of hide and seek the predator had just become the prey. Johnnie dived down behind it and aimed up at its vulnerable underbelly and fired a long, accurate burst of fire into the fuel tank. With no time for the pilot to bail out, the Messerschmitt exploded sending debris all around, and Johnnie had to bank steeply to the left to avoid the shrapnel. Now, low on fuel and ammunition, he headed in the direction of the English Channel.

"Dogsbody Four to Swallow," he called, "emergency homing please."

"Swallow to Dogsbody Four," came the reassuring reply, "steer three, four zero for home."

Constantly on the lookout for the enemy, Johnnie listened to the odd conversation against the crackle of static over the radio.

"Swallow to Dogsbody, come in Dogsbody – over?"

Johnnie waited for the reply from his leader but there was no answer.

"Swallow to Dogsbody. Do you require emergency homing? Come in Dogsbody – over!"

Johnnie waited a few seconds before he flicked the radio talk switch.

"Dogsbody Four to Swallow. We've had quite a scrap over

here. The last time I saw the Wing Commander he was firing on a 109."

"Thank you Johnnie," answered the controller solemnly.

By the time he returned to Westhampnett, Roy and Nick were waiting for him. In the maintenance bays all but two of the Spitfires were lined up in their usual places. One of the empty spaces was that of Bader's. Roy and Nick had already heard the news and were in a state of numbed disbelief. Nothing was said. A few minutes later Hugh returned from visiting Bader's wife, Thelma. When he saw Bader's redundant ground crew he turned his back. Johnnie reached up to put his hand on the tall man's shoulder.

"It's alright Hugh, what was it that Bader had always said? 'If a man can't cry, then he's not a really a man at all.' "

Inside the dispersal hut the intelligence officer, Scrine, was more businesslike as Johnnie, Hugh, Roy and Nick handed in their combat reports. If anyone knew Bader's whereabouts it would be Scrine. But he had nothing to report.

Out on the airfield, the late afternoon gave way to evening and the heavy scent of newly-mown grass hung in the cool air. Dusk brimmed over the tree tops and shadows lengthened. In the fading light, ground crews carried out their maintenance duties on the Spitfires in readiness for the following morning. Finally, having placed chocks under the wheels and canvas covers over the cockpits, one by one they left the airfield until only two crews remained.

The forlorn fitters and riggers peered expectantly in the direction of homecoming aircraft. When it was all but pitch black, Johnnie, Hugh, Roy and Nick climbed into the back of the airfield van and set off back to Tangmere. As the driver changed up through the gears Johnnie looked out through the back window at Bader's men, until they faded in the distance.

The following morning, the Tangmere Station Commander announced over the Tannoy that Bader was alive and well. He had been forced to bail out over France, picked up by the German Army and was held as a Prisoner of War. Cheering could be heard all around the airfield. The fact that he was still alive gave cause for great relief and celebration – but what now?

For Johnnie it was a personal low point. After all the months of struggling to get into the fight, it was Bader who had given him his first break. It was Bader who had recognised his talents and helped him overcome self doubt. It was Bader who had shown him that a true leader first wins the trust and loyalty of his men. But now he would never fly with him again. He was irreplaceable. Tangmere was darkened by a cloud of foreboding.

Things would never be the same again.

Chapter Six
WELBECK ABBEY

Within Fighter Command there was relentless competition between Squadrons as they each tried to elbow their way to the best airfields for fighting. Unsurprisingly, the High Command favoured those in the south east of England as they were closer to Europe. With Tangmere being more to the west, it had taken all of Bader's insistence and tenacity to keep his squadrons in battle. With him gone the place quickly returned to the quiet place that Johnnie had previously known. Once again he faced the angst of the lower pecking order but, thanks to Bader, he had at least been shown how to take on RAF High Command.

In addition he had won two kills in one mission which was an achievement that not even newly-promoted Group Captain Davidson could ignore. On his way to Davidson's office Johnnie noticed the ubiquitous green SS 90 sports car parked outside.

"Well done, Johnson," said Davidson casually. "Very unusual for someone of such little experience."

"Thank you, sir."

"Which is why you've been recommended for the Distinguished Flying Cross."

"Thank you, sir!"

Medals were things that Johnnie had never really considered before, but they could have their uses. Not even Davidson could deny the worth of a veteran pilot.

"Now that Bader is no longer here," he added, "High Command are making a few changes. The rate at which we are losing pilots means that we have to promote a number of you chaps – whether you are ready for it or not. You are to be promoted to Flight Lieutenant with immediate effect."

"Thank you, sir."

"And I'm sending you to Kirten Lyndsey. You leave tomorrow."

Kirten Lindsey was well known for being one of the most comfortable and well kept airfields. But, being situated in North Lincolnshire, its main purpose was for training and routine coastal patrols. Enemy fighters seldom bothered to venture so far north.

"With respect, sir – I'd rather stay here – near the fighting. I've only just..."

"You'll do as you're told Johnson," Davidson interrupted. "If you get bored, there's always plenty of Rhubarbs to do."

"When will I be returning to the Front, sir?"

"When I say so! Now there'll be a dinner for the Duke of Portland when you get up there."

"The Duke of Portland?"

"Yes, the squadron's Honorary Air Commodore. Make sure you look after him."

It was a shrewd move by Davidson. He had promoted Johnnie for his achievements and at the same time posted him out of the way to lead a section of four pilots to do very little.

When Johnnie arrived at Kirten with Roy and Nick they quickly became acquainted with pilots from many other nations. The Free French wore the uniform of the Armée de l'Air while the rest wore RAF uniforms bearing the shoulder flashes of Poland, Czechoslovakia, Canada, Australia, New Zealand, Rhodesia, South Africa, USA and Norway. Intrigued by men who had travelled far from their homes to risk their lives for another country, Johnnie made it his business to find out all he could about them.

Many of the European pilots had already suffered under Nazi occupation and had been forced to escape in their fighter aircraft for the relative safety of Britain. They longed for the days when they could return to liberate their countries and be reunited with loved ones. Their cause was the most desperate and touching. But for pilots of other nations, their countries were not occupied and were never likely to be. Those men had selflessly made it their mission to answer Britain's call and rid Europe of tyranny.

Johnnie found two 'bush' pilots one Canadian and one American particularly interesting. Johnnie had always considered the 'bush' to be the outback of Australia but these pilots had faced hardships of a different kind. They had travelled from the pioneering goldfields around Lake Winnipeg, Manitoba and the Red Lake, Ontario and their stories had Johnnie captivated. Often during their work at home they would fly alone for hundreds of miles over frozen lakes and forest. They lived in remote, unpopulated locations without any radio or mechanics to help them. In complete self-sufficiency they survived the coldest of winters in tents and fed themselves from the land. The threat of wolves and bears meant that they always carried rifles and they knew how to use them. Tough, dependable and fiercely proud, they were ideally equipped for the war in the air.

On the night of the dinner for the Duke of Portland, the cosmopolitan mix of pilots assembled in the Officer's Mess bar and Johnnie revelled in the atmosphere of international friendship. For one evening at least the serious side of their duties were suspended, and they all sat down together to an impressive candle-lit dinner. The wine flowed and the conversation was convivial even though language differences sometimes made it a little slow and stilted.

There was, however, a bizarre twist to it all. When Johnnie had worked as a surveyor in the coal mines in Staveley three years previously, he could never have imagined that one day he would ever be sitting next to his former employer. After dinner, attentive servants brought out port, brandy and cigars and the Duke engaged Johnnie in surprisingly genial conversation.

"Ever done any shooting, Johnnie? Apart from Huns of course!"

"Well I grew up in the country and I paid for my first shotgun by selling pigeon and rabbit to the local butcher."

"Good for you! You know the pheasant and partridge at Welbeck Abbey are quite good this season, why don't you bring some of your boys along sometime?"

"Thank you it would be a pleasure – and an opportunity for a spot of training."

"Training?" remarked the Duke. "Fighter pilots?"

With Roy, Nick and an enthusiastic and determined young pilot from New Zealand called Jeff, Johnnie drove the four of them to the Nottinghamshire estate in his Morris Eight. Welbeck Abbey was quite simply the biggest stately home any of them could ever have imagined. The tall entrance 'gate posts' were topped by statues of guardian lions and the tree-lined front courtyard was the size of two rugby pitches.

The main stone palace stood between two enormous adjoining wings both of which had high-pitched, green, copper roofs. The entire Abbey itself was surrounded by mature woodlands, fountains, a vast man-made lake and acres of open grassland. It was perfect game country. Feeling quite squat and insignificant amidst it all, Johnnie drove his little car to the 'front door' through which a butler emerged and he walked down the steps to greet them.

Out on the shoot the pilots were divided between other friends of the Duke who were eager to hear of their adventures, but first Johnnie showed Jeff the traditional safety codes. He pushed two long sticks into the ground to mark the limits of his aim to the left and the right. Then he reminded him that beyond the limits of the sticks the gun should always remain vertical.

"Got it?" ask Johnnie.

"Seems straightforward enough," said the New Zealander.

Satisfied that Jeff knew what he was doing, Johnnie left him and returned to the Duke's party. As promised, the birds were plentiful and lively and the day got off to a good start. But the Duke was still curious of Johnnie's training methods.

"And you say all this is good for a fighter pilot?"

"Absolutely," explained Johnnie. "You see most fighter pilots can shoot in a straight line . . . "

As he spoke Johnnie swapped his spent gun with the loader.

". . . bullets fall to the ground, of course, and so you have to aim up a bit to compensate . . . "

Then he spotted an incoming bird and raised the gun to his shoulder.

" . . . but take this bird on the turn," he continued. "If I aim straight at it, I'll miss. So I aim at where it is going."

BANG! The bird fluttered for a second and then hit the ground nearby with a thump.

"Basically the fighter is a flying gun and the enemy often twist and turn, just like game birds do."

The Duke was both intrigued and impressed with Johnnie's simple applied logic.

"So the policeman's son who has clawed his way up from a Sergeant Pilot in the Volunteer Reserve is now teaching RAF Pilot Officers how to shoot?"

"Well I wouldn't put it quite like that," said Johnnie.

"I would! And I think it's first class. You tell your men they are welcome to 'train' here for the rest of the season if they like."

"Thank you, m'Lord, I'd like to take you up on . . . "

Before Johnnie could finish his sentence he was startled by what he saw behind the Duke's shoulder. To his horror Jeff had got a pheasant in his sight and kept following it beyond the bounds of his shooting sticks. The bird jinked down and low until Jeff aimed straight in Johnnie's direction.

"Good God!" shouted Johnnie. "Look out!"

Just as Jeff opened up with both barrels, Johnnie grabbed the Duke, hurled him to the ground and fell on top of him. Lead shot hissed above them as they lay face to face on the ground. Johnnie was almost speechless with embarrassment.

"I'm awfully sorry m'Lord . . ." Johnnie got up and helped the Duke to his feet. " . . . I think the fighter pilot in him must have taken over. He didn't see the bird, he saw the enemy."

The Duke brushed himself off and dismissed the near fatal accident without a second thought.

"Oh don't mention it!" he said nonchalantly. "Come on, we'll have to get a move on if we're to get to the next drive."

It was a pleasant crisp day in late October. The sky was clear and the bright sun slanted on the autumnal colours of the trees and fields. The day passed without further incident, but Johnnie made sure he spent more time with his pilots teaching them safety as well as the country method of 'deflection' shooting. They all shot until nightfall and by the end of the day their kill rate had much improved. Tired, hungry and satisfied they retired to the hospitality of the Duke's residence.

That evening Johnnie and his men sat amidst the splendour of the old Abbey's dining hall. Feeling more than just a little self-conscious, the men were served an extravagant after-shoot fare of seasoned game, venison, fruit, ripened cheeses and no end of fine wine from the Duke's personal cellar. War-time rationing simply did not exist in this world. In Johnnie's mind he was taken back to the backstreets of the Duke's mining cottages in Staveley.

"Well," announced the Duke standing and raising his glass. "It's been a really wonderful day and I thank you all for your excellent company. Here's to six one six squadron."

All the men stood up, turned to the Duke and responded, "The six one six!"

As they sat down again, Jeff West peeped discreetly under

his dinner plate and turned to Johnnie and whispered.

"Christ! These plates are solid gold!"

"And I bet he doesn't wipe his arse on the *Daily Sketch*!" Johnnie whispered back.

"What?"

"Nothing."

A warm flickering glow from the log fire shone through the crystal glasses of port and brandy, while cigar smoke gently rose above the dining table. During conversation Johnnie mulled over the Duke's offer of more game shooting. It might just be enough to sharpen the marksmanship of his men and it would be good fun too. But rich food and drink in such opulent surroundings risked breeding a false sense of security. War could not be fought from the bloated cosiness of a fireside. Sooner or later they would be involved in some almighty scraps and Johnnie's men needed to be hungry and ready.

Chapter Seven
BUTCHER BIRD

While the pilots of 616 Squadron continued to 'train' at Welbeck, Johnnie phoned around in search of battle. Thousands of Canadian troops and pilots had started arriving in Britain and, although the USA was not formally at war with Germany, USAAF Eagle squadrons also started to arrive. And in the year after the Battle of Britain, the war in the air was now being taken over the English Channel by the Luftwaffe.

Security was tight and keeping up with any news of forthcoming missions was not easy. Notice for most of them was usually announced a couple of hours before they were scheduled to fly. But remembering Bader's tenacity and insistence, Johnnie kept 'in touch' with High Command and very occasionally he managed to get his section in on bomber escorts.

During one such mission they shadowed twenty Stirlings on a raid over Dunkirk. As usual the Nazi fighters were nowhere to be seen and Johnnie was just preparing to return home, when Kenway Radar called him up.

"Swallow to all sections, small formation of bandits. One five zero, five miles."

"Blue Leader to Swallow," Johnnie responded. "Any height?"

"Hard to tell Blue Leader . . . " Just then Roy cut in.

"There they are! Twelve of them, five o'clock high."

Nick confirmed the sighting with some considerable alarm.

"Bloody hell! They're fast! What the . . . what are they?"

"Careful, they could be Czechs or Poles..." Johnnie cautioned.

" . . . or Yanks? But I've never seen anything like these before."

"Whatever they are they're heading this way and they don't look friendly," said Roy.

Spotting their Swastika markings, Johnnie confirmed Roy's suspicions.

"They're Huns alright . . ." he said calmly, " . . . everyone break right. Keep them off the bombers."

Having been starved of a scrap for some weeks, the eager pilots turned to intercept the enemy fighters fully expecting to be evenly matched against Messerschmitt 109s. But the new aggressors flew towards them with such speed and agility that no one could line their guns up on them. When they opened up, they did so with blindingly awesome fire power; bright orange tracers flew all around. Straight away two Spitfires were hit and spiralled down.

"Bloody hell!" shouted Johnnie. "Everybody turn tight they won't be able to beat us in the turn!"

He was wrong. The Spitfires twisted and turned in desperation but they were out-turned, out-flown and out-gunned in every way. The skill and courage of Luftwaffe pilots was well known, but the new fighters were so devastatingly superior Johnnie was running out of tricks – except for one last chance. He had never seen a Nazi pilot fly fast and low.

"Get down! Right down!" he shouted. "Everybody hit the deck and get out!

The Spitfires dived down and the Nazi fighters gave chase. But at fifty feet they started to give up and when Johnnie's men were just a few feet above the waves of the English Channel the rest of them broke off and headed home.

Back at the dispersal hut the intelligence officer, Scrine, sat at a desk waiting for combat reports when Johnnie, Roy and Nick trudged in looking extremely shaken.

"What the hell happened to you lot?" he asked.

"We were hoping you could tell us that, "said Roy.

"They've got a new fighter," Johnnie added. "We tried everything, absolutely everything but we just couldn't get near them. And once they got fastened on behind us there was no shaking them off."

"Are you sure about this?" asked Scrine in astonishment. "This is the first we've heard about it."

"We're sure alright," said Johnnie emphatically. "I tell you this thing is bad news. Our old Spitfires are just not up to the job anymore. It really is as serious as that!"

Scrine opened his desk drawer and produced a large sheet of paper and a pencil.

"Look before we all get carried away with this, can you draw this new fighter for me? We've got to give the spooks some idea of what it is they're looking for."

As Johnnie began to draw, Roy and Nick added comments: "Square wing tips . . . round engine . . . thinner . . . that's more like it."

Finally, after a few aborted attempts, Johnnie produced a drawing of uncanny likeness.

"That's it!" said Johnnie. "That's the bastard that bounced us this morning."

Scrine gathered up the drawings and slipped them into his briefcase.

"I'll find out what the French Resistance can tell us. In the meantime I suggest you stay clear."

A few days later Scrine arrived at the main Spitfire factory in Birmingham. He walked straight in at the main entrance and past four long rows of Spitfires in various stages of construction. Weary factory workers, mainly women, were busy at riveting machines, lathes and benches. The factory radio blared out music and there was a smell of hot oil and aluminium.

In the upstairs office overlooking the shop floor, Scrine handed Johnnie's drawings to the factory manager, Stan Woodley. Woodley laid them on his desk next to a blueprint and a small model of a Spitfire.

"It's the Focke Wulf 190," said Scrine. "Apparently the Luftwaffe pilots call it the 'Butcher Bird' and according to our boys – that's exactly what it is."

"What's so good about it?" asked Woodley.

"Speed, agility, everything."

"So what else do we know? Got any photos? Anyone shot one down?"

"I'm sorry, that's it," admitted Scrine. "That's all we know, that, and the fact that we need a new fighter to tackle it."

Woodley stood bolt upright in astonishment.

"You're having me on!"

"No, not a bit!" answered Scrine.

Stan Woodley went over to the window and pointed down at the production floor.

"You see those people down there. They all work twelve hour shifts, seven days a week and now you want them to build something completely new, to beat something we know nothing about!"

Scrine walked over and stood next to Woodley. The view of the factory floor was indeed a vision of desperation, as scores of exhausted men and women worked nonstop in a non-stop race to keep Spitfire production rolling.

"I know Stan," said Scrine, "but this is serious. This new enemy Focke Wulf has got our boys completely pinned down."

"But a whole new fighter?" Woodley protested. "Even if we had the time to build one, now that poor old Reggie Mitchell's dead, who's going to design it?"

"Look," continued Scrine in exasperation, "if the Luftwaffe tried another full-on attack it would not be a rerun of the Battle of Britain, you know. With this thing they'd cut us to pieces. If Hitler decided to try and invade again, there would be nothing we could do to stop him. It doesn't get any worse than this. We need a new fighter and we need it now. It's as simple as that."

Woodley carried on gazing down at the workers.

"Okay. I'll see what I can do," he said with grim resolve. "But we need to know what it is we're supposed to beat. We need to get our hands on one of these 'Butcher Birds' – preferably in one piece!"

"I'll be in touch," said Scrine.

Scrine left the office and Woodley watched him through the office window as he made his way down the stairs, along the factory floor and out of the main door. After a few minutes of deep thought he sat behind his desk, checked Johnnie's drawing again and compared it to Reg Mitchells' original Spitfire design. About half an hour later he took a slide rule from out of his desk drawer and started to make calculations which he noted on the margin of the Spitfire blueprint. Picking up the model Spitfire, he balanced it on his finger. Then he took a small piece of putty and stuck it on its propeller and rebalanced it again. Keeping the model on the finger of one hand, with the other he picked up the telephone and pressed the scrambler button.

"Derby please, the Rolls Royce main office, Geoff Hives, thank you . . . Geoff? It's Stan at Castle Bromwich. Listen. That new engine of yours?"

"The Merlin sixty-one?" asked Hives on the other end of the line.

"Yes, that's the one. Is it any good?"

"Any good?" We've just put it in a Wellington bomber and you should see that thing go!"

"Can you bring one to Birmingham, I've got an idea."

On the 7 December 1941, Japan attacked the American naval base at Pearl Harbour, Hawaii. As a result the USA declared war on Japan and Germany and thousands of American troops and pilots started arriving in Britain. The landscape of southern England was transformed as every town, village and spare field was filled with American servicemen and hardware.

But it was the arrival of the Flying Fortresses of the mighty USAAF Eighth Air Force which caused the greatest excitement among the RAF fighter squadrons. The plan was to send huge formations of them on daytime raids all over northern Europe – and they were going to need fighter protection. It was a time of huge opportunity and anticipation and a new wave of anticipation swept over the south east England. And it was all happening at a time when Johnnie and his men were still up at Welbeck Abbey shooting game birds.

But not even the arrival of the Americans could stop the Focke Wulf 190 and almost overnight it was changing the direction of the war. Throughout the whole of the winter of 1941 and into the following spring the new Nazi fighters had almost complete freedom of the skies. With very little to stop them, they roamed at will over Britain attacking anything on the ground which took their fancy.

In the evening twilight of early June 1942 the pilot of a solitary Focke Wulf managed to get himself lost after attacking a bus load of aircraft factory workers in Bristol. Mistaking the Bristol Channel for the English Channel the pilot landed in error at RAF Pembrey in South Wales. As it came to a halt, it was watched by a duty pilot who grabbed a Very pistol and ran over to investigate. When the Nazi pilot opened the canopy, the duty pilot jumped onto the wing root and shoved the pistol under his nose.

The next day Scrine arrived at Pembrey and, joined by the Station Commander, they walked around the captured fighter and compared it to Johnnie's drawings. There was no mistaking the Focke Wulf 190 and there was not a mark on it.

"I want it kept under camouflage netting," said Scrine. "I'll arrange for transport in the morning."

In the test bay of the Spitfire factory in Birmingham, a new Merlin 61 engine had been fastened to a test frame and was being taken up to maximum power. The noise was deafening. Next to it stood a partially constructed prototype Spitfire. On Woodley's instruction, the engine was switched off and he went with Geoff Hives into the upstairs office.

On the wall of the office there were two blueprints of Spitfires, one of which had a longer nose. Stan Woodley pointed to it.

"According to Reg Mitchells' original plans, all we have to do is lengthen the nose by nine inches and then slot the new engine in."

"But Stan," said Hives with a look of concern, "this engine was built to pull a bloody great big bomber. It was never intended for a tiny little fighter like the Spit."

"I know," said Woodley, "that's why I want it!"

"Do you realise just how much power you're going to put into her? She's just not built for this. I mean yes, it could work. But it'll probably rip her apart!"

"Well there's only one way to find out, isn't there?"

Spitfires continued to be slaughtered at the hands of the Butcher Birds at an ever-increasing rate, and the number of fighter pilots was becoming critically low. In an urgent quest to find an answer to the problem, Scrine phoned the factory every day until eventually Woodley refused to take his calls.

The pressure on Woodley and Hives was immense. Within the confines of the factory they worked around the clock. Drawing after drawing and endless columns of calculations were produced, until eventually the two men agreed on a design. With the plans finalised, they handed the drawings over to a small, hand-picked team of fitters and engineers who set about the last stages of construction.

In the meantime Scrine arrived at Birmingham with the captured Butcher Bird and stood it next to the newly-developing Spitfire. Its sinister presence was a constant reminder of the urgency of the task. Supervised by Woodley and Hives the team drilled and riveted, fitted and refitted, and within just a few weeks Woodley's idea took shape in the form of the new 'Spitfire Nine'.

On the day of the engine test, the Spitfire had been moved out of the way of the shop floor and into the yard outside. The front cowling had been removed and two oil-covered, women fitters stood on step ladders as they made final adjustments to the fuel lines. In shirt sleeves, another woman fitter climbed into the cockpit. Finally the two fitters climbed down the ladders and moved them away.

Woodley gave the signal for engine start-up. In the still peace of the yard, the familiar pumping of the fuel priming and clicking of magneto switches could be heard as the fitter went through the start-up sequence. Finally she placed two fingers against the start buttons and looked over at Woodley. Woodley nodded back and she pressed them. The propeller began to turn, the fitter caught the ignition with a touch more throttle and the engine bellowed into life with an angry roar. Woodley and Hives glanced anxiously at one another. So far so good. Woodley made upward circling movements with his index finger, the fitter pushed her left hand against the throttle and the revs increased. Again and again Woodley signalled and the fitter pressed the throttle until she reached maximum power.

The Spitfire shuddered in her objection as the propeller blasted dust and debris out of the yard. After a few minutes Woodley and Hives nodded their approval at one another. Even as the colossal power of the mighty Merlin 61 was unleashed on her slender frame, she held firm. From beyond the grave Reggie Mitchell's original creation had stood the test. The old girl could take it.

Chapter Eight
ACE OF CLUBS

Throughout the summer of 1942, RAF fighter pilots and aeroplanes were destroyed in alarming numbers. Spitfire production just about kept pace with the need for replacements but newly-qualified pilots had very little time to gain experience before being sent to the front. Those who survived battle were promoted quickly and so Johnnie was sent to RAF Ludham in Norfolk to lead his first squadron. Being further south meant a greater chance of getting in on the fighting, but Johnnie still had reservations over pilot training and tactics.

American and Canadian troops continued to arrive in Britain, and with little else for them to do except train and wait, the Allied High Command decided it was time for them to prepare for an invasion of Europe. On the evening of 18th August, RAF commanders gathered together for a pre-mission briefing at West Malling.

The target was Dieppe. Five thousand Canadian and one thousand British troops were to launch an amphibious assault across the English Channel to 'soften up' the French port in readiness for the arrival of a liberating force. Dock yards, airfields and railways were listed for attack by ground troops, while RAF fighters were to provide air cover. At the same time American Flying Fortresses were to bomb the large enemy airfield at Abbeville. As the New Zealand Wing Commander known as 'Jamie' delivered the briefing, Johnnie leaned over to the pilot sitting next to him.

"I thought Monty said this lot should be called off?" he whispered.

The pilot shrugged and Jamie Jameson became somewhat hesitant as he continued.

"Now, air defences around Dieppe," he said unconvincingly, "are reported to be light."

Johnnie and the pilot next to him looked at one another in disbelief and other pilots shifted uncomfortably in their seats.

At first light the following morning, Johnnie led his squadron of twelve Spitfires over the English Channel. In the distance to his left he saw the tight box formation of Flying Fortresses heading for Abbeville. Immediately ahead, swarms of Spitfires and Hurricanes were already engaged in frantic dog fights with the Focke Wulf 190s. One after another, trails of smoke pointed to crippled RAF fighters as they fell out of the sky. Sooty black tufts of flak burst everywhere. Below, amphibious landing craft lined the surf and hundreds of dead bodies littered the beach and promenade. Over the radio the crackle of static was interrupted by the order of an unknown Wing Commander.

"Fight your way out!" he yelled. "All sections, just get out now!"

Trying to make some sense out of it all, Johnnie's eyes flashed around the sky in search of an opportunity to attack, and he found a large section of the enemy fighters above him to his right.

"Blue Leader to all sections," he called, "Watch those one nineties at one o'clock high. Don't let them near the Forts."

"Johnnie! One ninety on you," called Roy, urgently. "Twelve o'clock high, four hundred yards."

Johnnie reefed his Spitfire towards the incoming fighter as his boyhood hunting instincts kicked in. At four hundred yards it was a tricky shot. He aimed high and wide, pressed the firing button and orange tracer arced its way across the sky and fell onto the target. The wing was ripped off and it immediately started pouring black smoke. But as Johnnie watched it spinning down, Nick spotted an ambush.

"There's more coming down, Johnnie. Scores of the bastards."

Heavily outnumbered, Johnnie noticed Jamie Jameson's Spitfire high in the distance.

"Jamie, we've got fifty plus bandits closing from inland. Twelve o'clock high. Can you spare any help?"

With remarkable calmness Jamie replied amidst the sound of his machine guns.

"Sorry, Johnnie. Bit busy over here!"

The enemy closed in and Johnnie was forced to call the break.

"Here they come! All sections break now!"

Johnnie's section broke tight in all directions but the Focke Wolfe's turned tighter and gave chase. The sun swung blindingly back and forth across Johnnie's face as he threw the Spitfire around in a frantic bid to escape. After an inverted power dive he levelled out just feet above the ground and he was free. Free, but alone in a hostile sky. All he could hear were the distant calls of leaders telling their men "to get out". With no hope of forming up with any wingmen he knew he would not last long on his own and he turned for the Channel.

On the outskirts of Dieppe, Johnnie was just about to make his last dash for the safety of Britain, when above him he spotted a solitary Focke Wulf 190 which looked lost. Abandoning caution he could not resist such an inviting target and he climbed up towards it on its blind side. But as he turned for the attack the enemy pilot spotted him and turned to counter attack. As the 190 got closer Johnnie noticed it had an orange propeller spinner and there was an ace of clubs logo beneath the cockpit.

The two aircraft turned around each other as they both tried to get behind into an attack position. But the 'Ace of Clubs' held the tighter turn and was soon on Johnnie's tail. He pulled the Spitfire round as hard as he could, draining the blood from his head and his vision turned to grey. But it was no use, the Focke Wulf 190 was by far the superior aircraft and Johnnie could not outturn his opponent. If he did not find some form of cover it would only be a matter of seconds before the enemy would be in a position to take a lethal shot. He looked below to see the church steeples and rising columns of smoke of Dieppe. They were his only chance. Diving down, he twisted in and out of the smoke and steeples to give himself vital seconds of thinking time. But his every switch and turn was matched by the Ace of Clubs. Out in the English Channel a Royal Navy destroyer was surrounded by several other smaller ships.

With the Ace of Clubs moving into perfect attack position, Johnnie suddenly pulled hard right, flew down as low as he could and headed straight towards the destroyer at full throttle. The Focke Wulf 190 followed and closed the gap.

On board the destroyer the anti-aircraft gun crew spotted two unidentified aircraft heading towards them and began shooting. At the same time the enemy pilot opened fire and orange tracer flashed both ways just inches above Johnnie's cockpit. He pushed the throttle into the emergency setting and when he was just feet away from the destroyer he pulled hard on the stick and his Spitfire narrowly cleared the radio mast. Once over the other side of the ship Johnnie dived back down and turned to face his opponent. But he did not appear.

Sweating and panting Johnnie made a couple of clearing turns to make sure he was alone. Recognising the elliptical wings of the Spitfire, the gun crew of the destroyer stopped shooting and Johnnie set a course for home.

He returned to Ludham, landed on the welcoming turf, and weaved his way towards the ground crew who waited in his maintenance bay. But much to his surprise the usual rigger and fitter had been joined by an excited camera crew. He taxied to a halt, switched the engine off, flicked the magneto switches and the gyro compass whined down. When he climbed out of his cockpit a camera was pointed at him, a microphone boom swung over his head and he was confronted by a chatty journalist.

"Any luck up there today, Johnnie?" asked the journalist.

"One, maybe two I think," said Johnnie. "To be confirmed."

"Well done. That makes you an ace! Tell us, Sailor Malan is the top scorer so far. Do you think you can beat him?"

"Well, Sailor Malan is not the enemy. If I want to beat anyone it's the Luftwaffe."

But the journalist persisted, "Of course! But do you think you can be the top scorer?"

Still shaken after his ordeal, Johnnie struggled to conceal his irritation.

"It's not about my score or anyone else's, it's about the total. The more we all knock down together, the better chance we will have of winning."

After a couple of more questions Johnnie excused himself and walked away rubbing the back of his stiffened neck.

A few days later in a cinema in Norwich, Paula Ingate, a fire service worker, sat with a friend watching a Pathé newsreel of Johnnie's recent interview.

"But you're quite a rising star, Johnnie. What's it like now that you are a Squadron Leader?" asked the journalist.

"I wouldn't want to do anything else," Johnnie replied.

Flickering cones of light from the back of the cinema shone through the rising coils of cigarette smoke as Paula's friend leaned over and whispered in the dark.

"What a dish!"

Paula just gazed and said nothing.

At Brooklands Airfield Woodley, Hives and Air Vice-Marshall Stevens had gathered to watch the new Spitfire Nine being tested against the Focke Wulf 190. The two fighters took off side by side and flew into the distance. In the first fast low pass the Focke Wulf 190 still had the advantage and took the lead. Stevens turned to Woodley in exasperation.

"Stan, I already know it's faster than the Spit!" and he turned to leave.

"No, wait," said Woodley. "We're not finished. Just watch!"

At the end of the low pass the two fighters entered a steep

climb. The Spitfire caught up and overtook. After a punishing aerobatic display the two aircraft engaged in a mock dog fight. Each time the Spitfire turned tighter and managed to get into an attacking position. Finally in a race at high altitude the Spitfire overtook and won.

Stevens watched in silence and then raised his binoculars to watch the two fighters on their final approach. Woodley and Hives looked at one another anxiously.

"Tighter turn," said Stevens to himself, "faster climb and, if we keep out of trouble just above the ground, we've got them in a straight race."

"Exactly," said Woodley with pride, "a thoroughbred, wouldn't you say?"

"You may just be right there," said Stevens, "and a thoroughbred takes some handling – not a job for the average pilot."

He slotted his binoculars back into their case and turned to Woodley.

"When can we place an order?"

Chapter Nine
PAULA

Lack of intelligence and poor planning by the Allied High Command had turned the raid on Dieppe into a bloody and unnecessary disaster. Over half the ground troops were killed and many of the survivors were badly injured. Most of them were Canadian. That such an avoidable gamble should have been permitted to go ahead in the first place left Johnnie in a gloomy malaise.

It was time to spend some leave on a good night out and so he phoned Hugh and they met up in Norwich. After a crawl of a few pubs they made their way to the Sampson and Hercules Ballroom where they found an empty table at the edge of the dance floor. After a couple more drinks Johnnie noticed a couple getting up to dance over the other side of the room. The pretty dark-haired girl with her inescapable smile looked somehow familiar, and as they glided by Johnnie was filled with envy.

"Lucky bastard!" he said under his breath.

"I don't think he's actually with her, Johnnie," said Hugh. "I didn't see a ring on her finger."

"No?"

Johnnie was intrigued. The music stopped and all the dancers applauded.

"You know Hugh, I'm sure I've seen her photograph in the newspapers."

"Who is she?"

"I can't remember her name but I'm sure she won the Miss Norwich Beauty Contest.

When the band leader announced that the following dance would be an 'excuse me' Johnnie stood up, extinguished a cigarette and smoothed his uniform.

"I'll go and ask her."

He waited for a suitable moment and just as the couple passed nearby again he tapped the man on the shoulder.

"Excuse me," he asked politely. "Would you mind if I finished this dance with her?"

The man looked unsure, but after a moment the girl agreed and reassured her partner.

"It's alright I'll see you later."

Johnnie took the girl in his arms.

"He doesn't look too happy!" he said.

"That's Tom. He's an old schoolfriend of my brother's. He told my dad he'd look after me tonight."

"So he's not your sweetheart then?"

"No, I've known him for years."

As they started to dance the girl looked at Johnnie inquisitively.

"I'm Johnnie, what's your name?"

"Paula, Paula Ingate."

"I'm sure I've seen that name somewhere before," said Johnnie. "Were you in the Miss . . . "

Then Paula suddenly blurted it out.

"Now I know where I've seen you," she said excitedly. "In the cinema on the Pathé News. You're that fighter Ace from Dieppe!"

Johnnie smiled uncomfortably, "Crikey! Word certainly gets around!"

The band played another number, but Johnnie and Paula did not even notice which dance it was or even where they were, it didn't matter. They just talked and talked and laughed.

In an instant the evening was all but over. With the lights dimmed, the glitter ball turned slowly in the spotlight and thousands of pools of light swirled around them. Johnnie was utterly smitten. But suddenly the spell was broken.

"And now ladies and gentlemen," announced the band leader, "please take your partners for the last waltz."

Paula looked at her watch with alarm. She gently broke her dancing embrace and looked over to the cloakrooms anxiously. She was about to go and Johnnie knew he was about to lose her. For a moment he almost panicked.

"Oh stay for the last dance – please!"

"No, no – I can't, "insisted Paula. "I must meet my brother. He'll be waiting by the cloakrooms."

"Can't I take you home?" asked Johnnie. "My car's outside."

Paula was just nineteen, and yet standing in front of her pleading not to be rejected was an RAF Squadron Leader and national hero. He was quite the most handsome man she had ever met, dressed in the most glamorous uniform in the world and he wanted her.

"I'm sorry I can't. I promised my dad that my brother would take me home. But I'll be here next week!"

"I might not be here tomorrow, never mind next week," insisted Johnnie. "I'm due to be sent away soon. Please?"

The fear and excitement was intoxicating. Paula's heart pounded. How could she take a chance on a man she had only just met?

"Alright then," she said, "but I need to tell my brother first."

Outside the nightclub, service men and women and civilians emptied out through the revolving doors of the exits. Couples linked arms and walked. Less fortunate singles walked or waited for buses. Johnnie and Paula walked arm in arm around the corner and along the darkened street to his little Morris. He opened the passenger door for her and, once she had tucked her skirt around her legs, he closed it again and walked around to the driver's side. In, door closed and key in the ignition. It was time to go. But right away? Paula's glance was nervously inviting. Johnnie turned and leaned towards her.

"I've never kissed on the first date," she whispered breathlessly.

For a moment Johnnie looked playfully rebuffed.

"Until now," he said with a smile – that irrepressible, playful smile.

By the time they reached the Officer's Mess bar it was 3.00 a.m. Paula would be going home late. The wreckage of indoor rugby was strewn all around. Three very drunk pilots were slumped in armchairs with their jackets unfastened. One pilot lay unconscious on the floor snoring loudly. Another unconscious pilot was perched on a stool with his head and arms sprawled on top of the bar amid the empty glasses, spilt beer and cigarette ends. Johnnie suppressed his grin at the all too familiar sight. Paula was quietly shocked as she picked her way delicately around the debris. Johnnie took her hand and led her to the bar.

"Pull up a body and sit down," he said.

Johnnie gave the pilot sitting at the bar a gentle push and he slithered off the end and flopped onto the floor like a slaughtered beast in an abattoir. Still holding Paula with one hand, Johnnie swept the bar clear and, with the smooth flourish of a posh waiter, he offered her the vacated bar stool.

"Madame?"

Paula settled herself at the bar and Johnnie walked around behind it. Next to the optics there was a barrel beer glass full of coins. Johnnie reached up to the glass, stuffed a ten shilling note into it and took out some change. He poured a couple of gin and tonics and as he served one to Paula he looked around at the comatose pilots lying amidst the battered remnants of the evening's sport.

"Nightcap anyone?" he sniggered.

One of the pilots slumped in an armchair forced his eyelids open.

"A girl!" he slurred with Etonian vowels. "Old Johnnie's brought a girl into the mess!"

"Well spotted old boy! Meet Paula."

Johnnie leaned his elbows on the bar, clinked glasses with the girl he was falling in love with and gazed with affection.

"See that," he said, "instant recognition. Keen eyes these chaps!"

Paula leaned forwards slowly. Johnnie moved to meet her kiss but she stopped short.

"Johnnie? When you get your new posting, will you come and see me?"

Johnnie paused and thought for a moment.

"What's the matter? Don't you like it here?"

Castletown, North East Scotland, 27 October 1942
Johnnie led his squadron into land on the remote, windswept

airfield. Two at a time the Spitfires taxied in and came to a stop in a neat row. One by one the pilots stood up in their cockpits and looked around in disbelief. The vast, rugged, open country had a beauty all of its own. It was the type of beauty, which at any other time, Johnnie would have been content to explore in search of game.

With the arrival of the Americans, the war had stepped up several gears and RAF Spitfires and American fighters escorted the USAAF Flying Fortresses on daily raids over Europe. Word of the high-performing new Spitfire Nine was beginning to filter around Fighter Command and it was even rumoured that it could knock down a Focke Wulf 190. At the time of the greatest excitement and anticipation, Johnnie was further away from the action than he had ever been. He had already waited too long and he could no longer contain his frustration.

He climbed out of his cockpit, borrowed a nearby airfield car and raced off in the direction of the control office. Inside the office a startled sergeant jumped up and saluted as Johnnie burst in and angrily picked up the phone.

"Squadron Leader Johnson. Yes, Bentley Priory please. Yes, as a matter of fact it is urgent!"

Johnnie arrived at the gates of Bentley Priory in his Morris and had his papers checked by the guard who promptly saluted and opened the barrier. Standing in the section of the car parked reserved for staff was Davidson's Jaguar SS80. In the ante-room to Davidson's office Johnnie stood straining his ears to listen in on the muffled conversation going on behind the closed door. The voices stopped and there were footsteps on the carpeted floor. The office door opened and a red-faced group captain emerged.

"The AVM will see you now, but you better make it quick, he's busy!"

Johnnie marched into Davidson's office, came to attention in front of his desk and saluted. Davidson remained seated and acknowledged the salute with his usual vague nod.

"At ease, Johnson," he sighed. "I understand you want to see me about your posting to Castletown. Apparently you disagree."

Johnnie had rehearsed his case and began with great tact.

"Well, with respect sir, I understood that it was our turn at the Front."

"Your turn!?"

"Yes sir," continued Johnnie. "You see my men have trained very hard . . ."

Uninterrupted, Johnnie listed every item with meticulous detail. Every posting, every ground attack training session, every aerial combat training session, every deflection shooting practice and all the weeks and months of waiting and waiting.

". . . and so, sir, that is why we thought it was our turn in the south east."

Davidson paused, engaged Johnnie with a steady eye and spoke slowly and deliberately.

"Squadron Leader, you've finally managed to land Spitfires without crashing and you're even emerging as something of a marksman. That doesn't mean you can come in here and question my decisions! It would appear this Pathé News pantomime has gone to your head. Now, go back to Castletown and tell your men that they are to remain there until further orders."

"In that case, sir you wouldn't mind if I take a little overdue leave?"

"What you do with your own time is up to you, Johnson. Good day."

On the 14 November 1942, after a brief engagement, twenty-five-year-old Johnnie married his young bride in Norwich Registry Office. His friend Hugh Dundas was his best man and Roy and Nick were among the other guests at the Haymarket Hotel.

At first Paula's father had been deeply suspicious of Johnnie. Pilots were well known for drinking and womanising and were not considered by many to be reliable husband material. But Johnnie was in love and he went to great lengths to reassure Mr. Ingate that he would look after his daughter. And true to his word Johnnie convinced Paula that an RAF station was far too dangerous a place for her to live. She would either stay in Norwich with her parents or in Melton Mowbray with his.

After the wedding breakfast, Johnnie sat in a big armchair with Paula on his knee while celebrations began around them. Paula rested her head against his shoulder and as he slipped his arm around her waist she admired her wedding ring.

"Johnnie?" asked Paula thoughtfully. "What about a honeymoon?"

"I know just the place."

Chapter Ten
PARTY TOWN

Saturday 21 November 1942, Blackpool Pleasure Beach
The huge bicycle chain of the Big Dipper ride clunked rhythmically as it hauled the cars up the wooden, latticed ramp. Johnnie grinned mischievously; Paula was filled with trepidation. At the top they crept slowly around the ornamental 'onion' and then plunged sickeningly down the high, steep track to a chorus of screams and clattering wheels. With one arm around Paula's shoulders, Johnnie strangely had nothing else do to. No controls to kick and push, no enemy over his shoulder to worry about, no 'empty' fuel gauge and no pilots to bring home. This was one ride in the sky which was completely carefree.

Britain's industrial and coastal towns were being battered by the Luftwaffe but, strangely, Blackpool was virtually untouched. Recognised as a safe haven it had become the party town and black market capital of the north. Servicemen and women and civilians alike flocked in their thousands to spend their hard earned cash.

For many city folk, the slaughter of nightly bombing had turned life into a lottery and no one knew if they would survive to the next day. Attitudes were being forced to change and the old Victorian values of chastity and restraint gave way to a new sexual revolution. In Blackpool, the promenades and pubs were filled with reunited couples sharing precious time together, while singles indulged in alcohol-fuelled flirting as they searched for someone to share a bed with. With so much spending going on, Spivs from all over the country brought in rationed food and clothes. For anyone who had the money, there was nothing that could not be bought on the streets of Blackpool.

In and out, in a pocket-emptying tour of shops and chemists, Johnnie showered Paula with gifts of perfumes, soaps, silk stockings and a handbag. Finally they went in search of 'that dress' for the evening ahead. In 'Tipping of Chenley' Paula twirled in a slinky, black evening gown which called out to Johnnie – 'buy me'! At the glass-top counter the shop assistant surreptitiously produced a drawer full of silk scarves. Paula unfurled a dark green one and made a cravat out of it around Johnnie's neck. He gave a look of mild disapproval.

"For when you're flying," she said. "It'll remind you of me."

On the ground floor of the old department store they were heading for the exit when Paula spotted a baby display featuring a handsome 'Swan' pram. She unlinked her arm from Johnnie's, walked over and rocked it cheekily.

"Come on," said Johnnie with a wry smile, "we've got the rest of our honeymoon yet!"

Back on the promenade, they strolled arm in arm past the North Pier. Outside the theatre at the end of the pier was a huge picture of a man dressed in a blue blazer and white flannel trousers. He wore a white straw hat, small, thick, round glasses and smoked a cigar. The sign next to it said, 'The Dave Morris Laughter Show'. They stopped, thought about it, and then carried on back to the Empress Hotel.

That evening started with a visit to the casino. Inside were a great many young men who were busy showing off to their girlfriends. Although most of them looked fit enough to fight, none were in uniform. Instead they wore expensive suits and ties and seemingly had no end of cash. It was a scene which was not to Johnnie's taste and so they left.

Inside Yates's Wine Bar the room was packed with servicemen and football supporters. The floor was covered with sawdust and the ceiling was obscured by a dense cloud of cigarette smoke. In the middle of the crowd a man with an impish face stood on a chair and clung onto a cast iron pillar. As he led the room in a loud rendition of *Sylveste* he swayed back and forth, spilling beer.

"You've heard about the big strong man, he lives in a big caravan . . . "

"This is more like it!" yelled Johnnie down Paula's ear.

In stunned disbelief Paula followed Johnnie as he took her by the hand and squeezed his way to the bar. Within minutes he was served and joined in the singing enthusiastically.

"That's my brother Sylveste – what's he got? A row of forty medals on his chest . . ."

Earlier Paula had bathed with her expensive soap, spent nearly an hour on her hair and makeup, slipped on her new stockings and dress and prepared for the honeymoon evening of her life. Johnnie was on a mission to get pissed. When he came to his favourite line he turned to her and sang loudly with a manic excited smile.

" . . . *it takes all the army and the navy, to put the wind up Sylveste!"*

Paula stood silently in front of him, young, delicate and gorgeous and the only girl in the room.

Johnnie was stopped dumbstruck in his tracks. He put his half-finished pint down on a shelf and Paula put her wine glass next to it. He slipped a big protective arm around her shoulders and they left.

In the gloriously ostentatious Victorian atrium of the Tower Ballroom, the floor was full. It was still early and there was plenty of time for dancing and so Johnnie found a small, empty table in a quiet corner and they sat down. He ordered some drinks and at last they were alone together in the crowd. Johnnie held Paula's hand under the table.

"Johnnie?" Paula began.

"Yes, darling?"

"You know this afternoon when we were in . . ."

Just then the waiter arrived with the drinks and as Johnnie stood up to reach into his trousers pocket he collided with a man in a blue blazer who was about to sit down. Johnnie nearly knocked the man off his feet but caught him before he fell over.

"Steady on!" quipped the man. "You're going to get us both thrown out!"

"Terribly sorry," said Johnnie.

As he spoke the man strained to examine Johnnie's face. Johnnie recognised the man straight away.

"Are you Dave?" asked Johnnie. "Dave Morris?"

"The same!" said Dave with equal disbelief. "Johnnie Johnson! The Spitfire Ace – and this must be your lovely girlfriend. I've read all about you. You too Paula."

Johnnie and Dave shook hands warmly and Dave bent down to kiss Paula on the cheek. He invited the couple to join him at his table and, concealing her disappointment, Paula stood up and changed tables. As they sat down a man in a Royal Navy uniform patted Dave on the back and he turned to shake hands with yet another of his fans. Paula whispered discreetly in Johnnie's ear.

"Oh really Johnnie, this is going to ruin our evening."

"Don't worry we'll get up and go for the next dance."

The band struck up loudly and Dave could only make himself heard by speaking into Paula's ear. He was every bit a natural comedian and possessed an effortless, unthreatening charm.

As the night passed, the three became friends as Dave treated Johnnie and Paula to their own personal comedy show. But despite his poor eyesight Dave could see that Paula was troubled. Her laughter was sometimes nervous and her smile hesitant. Although she tried to hide her longing for Johnnie, her hand permanently sought the reassurance of his. There was no disguising it from Dave, she needed to talk. Then a slow waltz was announced.

"Look you two!" said Dave, "it's your honeymoon. You shouldn't spend the evening with a sad old bachelor like me. Why don't you go and dance?"

"Why not?" said Paula.

Johnnie took her hand and they stepped onto the dance floor.

"What's wrong?" asked Johnnie.

"Nothing darling, I'm perfectly happy . . . "

". . . . but?"

"Well, why is it too early," she asked, "for a family, I mean?"

"Paula, you know how I feel. I don't want to be an absent father. I want to be there to see our children grow up."

"When then?"

"I don't know. Who knows how long this war will last?"

"The end of the war! That could take years!"

"Paula, please. Let's talk about it later."

At the end of the last dance the ballroom started to empty, but before they left Dave had one last gesture.

"You must join me for dinner sometime."

"Oh, we'd love to," said Paula, "but I'm afraid we've got to go back tomorrow."

"Oh no, that's terrible," said Dave."

He reached into his jacket pocket and produced two tickets.

"Look," he insisted, "here are two tickets for the show – for next time you're in Blackpool. Be sure you look me up."

By the following Tuesday, Johnnie and Paula were back in Melton Mowbray and they went to visit his parents. When they arrived Johnnie's dad presented him with a Royal Mail bag. Much to Paula's surprise and consternation it was stuffed full of cards and love letters from admiring girls all over Britain, some even smelled of perfume. The nation had been thrilled by the Pathé News reel which had captured the story of the dashing Squadron Leader's adventures over France and they were eager for more.

The following day Johnnie returned to Caithness.

Chapter Eleven
CANADIANS

Once back in his northern exile, Johnnie trained his men hard throughout the winter months. Teamwork, discipline and commitment were his priorities and together they set a record for the highest number of rounds ever fired at ground targets. Although they had arrived too late for the salmon season they were well received by friendly locals who often advised and guided them during game hunts. The landlord and landlady of the Dunnet Hotel also made them very welcome, and the meat of the beasts they shot often found their way onto their dining tables. Whenever the squadron was invited, Johnnie always insisted that men of all ranks should eat and drink together. With combat skills honed and friendships bonded, his men were keyed up and ready for the real thing.

In January 1943 Johnnie's squadron was transferred back to Tangmere. But during the two years after his first encounter with Bader, the ever-present Focke Wolfe 190s had changed everything. The daylight bombing raids over Europe by Flying Fortresses were escorted by both American and RAF fighters but in the dog fighting, which took place in defence of the bombers, a great many were lost to Focke Wulf 190s. Throughout it all Johnnie managed to keep the morale of his men high, but they simply did not possess an aeroplane that was up to the challenge.

At RAF Fighter Command at Bentley Priory the prospects

of new aeroplanes, new pilots and the ever-shifting sands of war were causing friction between the traditionalists and the modernizers. In the early production days of the new Spitfire Nine there were only a limited number available, and the big question was who should be the first to fly them? To the Auxiliary traditionalists, family and school guaranteed more reliable types and they considered themselves to be the most suitable to take first delivery. The modernisers took the view that as the Spitfire Nine was the RAF's only hope of taking on the Focke Wulf 190s, proven ability should take priority over pedigree.

The wing at RAF Kenley in Surrey was widely regarded as being one of the best in Fighter Command and in early 1943 it was made up of newly-trained pilots from Canada. The Canadians had a reputation for being skilful and courageous pilots, but they were also rowdy and ill-disciplined and were not taken seriously by the traditionalists. After all most Canadians had never even ridden in a fox hunt.

Late one evening at Bentley Priory, Air Vice-Marshall Davidson and Air Vice-Marshall Stevens lit cigars and adjourned to the lounge after dinner. Stevens poured two large brandies and handed one to Davidson. The two men sat opposite one another by the flickering glow of the fireside. It had fallen to Stevens to find a replacement Wing Commander for the Canadians at Kenley and he enquired of Davidson's men.

"Bloody rabble those Canadians," complained Davidson. "Sorry! Can't help you!"

"I've been reading Johnson's operations record," hinted Stevens.

"Johnson! No, no. Wrong sort!"

"What is it with you and him?"

"He came in through the back door of the Volunteer Reserve – we know nothing about him – but we do know that he's a Squadron Leader and his face is on every newspaper!"

"Not jealous are you, Howard?" quipped Stevens. "You know it was me who put Pathé News onto him. I thought he did a pretty good job."

Ever since that first interview all those years ago Stevens had been impressed by Johnnie's enterprising way of funding his own flying lessons. In Johnnie, Stevens saw a practical man of the land, a problem solver and he had followed his progress from afar. He knew all about the crashes, the shoulder injury and the setbacks and he had watched each time as Johnnie had picked himself back up. He had also read all his combat reports and followed the training programmes he had designed, even at Welbeck Abbey. To him Johnnie was more than just a fighter pilot, he was a natural leader.

Stevens also had a vision. If the new Spitfire Nines were as deadly as reports had suggested, and if the bush pilots of Canada were as tough and resourceful as he had heard, then Spit Nines – flown by Canadians and led by the wily and inventive hunter from the fields of Leicestershire – it would be a lethal combination. To Stevens it would be a match made in heaven and he was not for giving up on his man.

"You seriously want to put a man like Johnson in charge of thirty-six pilots!"protested Davidson. "Canadian pilots at that! Those rough buggers need a proper leader. Firm hand on the reins!"

"Well I've been following his form. He's trained his men

well, their morale is high and he never gives up. I think the Canadians will like him."

"They'll eat him alive!"

"Yes, but Howard, that would be his problem, not yours."

"I don't know what's happening these days," complained Davidson. "There was a time when we had reliable chaps from reliable families. Now anything goes."

Stevens let his old friend simmer for a good few minutes before making his last move.

"Look, I tell you what . . ." he said disarmingly, " . . . if you let me have him I'll take him off your hands – for good. If it doesn't work out I can always send him back to Caithness out of the way. You wouldn't ever have to worry about him again."

Davidson pondered further as he sipped his brandy. He drew on his cigar and pouted a large plume of thick, blue smoke.

"You'll keep him out of my way?" he asked.

"Absolutely!"

Davidson stood up, refilled his glass, walked over to Stevens with the decanter and topped up his glass.

"I think you're wrong . . ." he said at last, ". . . but you can have him. He's yours!"

On the morning when he took the telephone call from the High Command, Johnnie was immediately suspicious of the line of questioning by the nosey Group Captain who wanted to know too much about his stay up in Caithness. Johnnie suspected another move to nowhere.

"Just a moment," said the Group Captain.

Johnnie waited anxiously as he listened to the clicking

noises of the telephone line as he was transferred to another number. Eventually he heard Stevens' voice.

"Morning Johnnie, Stevens here."

"Morning, sir."

"I hear you've had a bit of a rest up there. Did you get there in time for the salmon season?"

"Oh yes, sir," he lied, "couldn't have been better! We've all had a really good long rest."

"Good, because I'm promoting you to Wing Commander."

"Wing Commander!"

"You're to take charge of the Canadians at Kenley."

Canadians! He remembered them from Kirten Lyndsey and had often wondered what it would be like to lead them.

"They've got the new Spitfire Nines and they're expecting you down there tomorrow. Good luck!"

Just like the reorganisation that followed Bader's capture, a widespread reshuffle was in progress. However, instead of being sent to shoot game birds, this time the dice had rolled in Johnnie's favour. But so rapid were all the new changes that there was only one night for saying farewells. In the Unicorn Pub at Chichester the bar was full of pilots of various ranks. Hugh, Roy and Nick had made the journey especially to celebrate Johnnie's promotion and in between swilling back copious amounts of beer they sang their way through all the old songs and the new. Johnnie had taught them the words to the song he learned in Blackpool and they were half way through a loud rendition of *Sylveste* when he looked through the bar room door to see that the telephone in the hallway was free.

Although Paula had not created a fuss about children Johnnie knew that she was incurably broody. Having come to terms with the prospect of being an absent father he had arranged to meet her that following weekend. But the unexpected posting meant that it would all have to be cancelled and telling her would not be easy. He squeezed his way through the tightly-packed bodies and made his way into the hallway. He put his pint down on the telephone pay box and dialled Paula's number.

At Paula's parent's house everyone was asleep when the phone rang. Knowing it would probably be Johnnie, Paula abandoned the warmth of her bed, wrapped herself in her dressing gown and hurriedly shivered her way down the stairs. When she picked up the receiver all she could hear on the other end of the line was the 'last orders' bell ringing to the accompaniment of '*He's got an arm, like a leg – a ladies leg!*'

"Hello?" she said sleepily.

In the best way he could, Johnnie shouted above the racket in the background.

"Paula, it's me Johnnie!"

"Where are you?"

"In the pub. We're all being moved on," he slurred, "and we're having a little farewell party. Can't you hear it?

"Yes, they're singing that dreadful song again!"

"Listen darling. I can't tell you where I'm going . . . but I can't make next weekend . . I have to leave tomorrow, I'm so sorry."

"Oh, why can't you make it?"

"Well, you see darling, I've been promoted. I'm a Wing Commander!"

"Why can't they promote you after our weekend?"

PART 2
LEADERSHIP

Chapter Twelve
TACTICS

On 19 March 1943, nursing a hangover and with his new gundog Sally the Labrador curled up on the passenger seat of his Morris, Johnnie drove to his new job at RAF Kenley. As he contemplated his new responsibilities his mind became filled with conflicting emotions. What was he getting into? The freedom and satisfaction of making his own decisions, or the loneliness of command?

At the gatehouse the guard gave Johnnie directions and he drove around the perimeter track towards the Officer's Mess. Having been used to working with mixed nationalities he had always enjoyed the rivalry and humour that they brought, but this was to be different. He was an Englishmen and he was about to take charge of an exclusively Canadian wing.

Almost immediately he felt as if he had driven straight into an unwelcoming foreign land. The buildings and the layout all looked familiar enough but the atmosphere could not have been more different. Groups of men pitched baseball lazily, only stopping momentarily to watch Johnnie as he drove by. Caps, if worn, sloped at casual angles. Pilots had hands in their pockets and chewed gum – with their mouths open! No one turned upright to face him and there were no salutes.

Outside the Officer's Mess a group of pilots looked on as Johnnie arrived. In the middle of them was an American Squadron Leader known simply as 'Dan'.

Johnnie parked his car and got out, followed excitedly by Sally. As he took his cases from out of the boot, Dan made his assessment.

"I guess that's what the Limey's call an automobile!"

Scarcely out of earshot, the rest of the pilots sniggered.

The following day Johnnie's new senior officer, Group Captain Bill McCord, took him on a tour of the airfield. Apart from the Squadron Leaders he was about to command, the new acquaintance he was most eager to meet was the Spitfire Nine. After a brief update on handling and performance Bill took him into one of the hangers where Dan, the inevitable Scrine, and Squadron Leader Syd Bradford were waiting.

"There she is!" said Bill with great excitement, "ain't she a beauty?"

It was a Spitfire, much the same as any other Spitfire.

"This it then?" asked Johnnie cautiously. "This is the new one? The Spitfire Nine."

"Yep!" said Bill. "Something wrong? You want me to show you around her?"

"No, no. That's alright," said Johnnie thoughtfully.

Except for the slow echoing clicks of Johnnie's footsteps, the hanger was silent. Dan and Syd looked at Johnnie and then at one another in suspicion. There in front of them all was the RAF's last chance and big hope and there was the man who was going to be in charge. So where was his excitement and enthusiasm? As Johnnie rounded the other side of the propeller Bill broke the silence as if spouting a brief piece of salesmanship

"She's got the new Merlin 61 engine! A real monster!"

Johnnie bent down and looked at Bill from under the nose.

"Yes. Hence the longer engine bay, I can see that."

Then he carried on his inspection, smoothing his hands over her wings and body. He stopped at the tail and waggled the rudder back and forth.

"But apart from that," he said conspiratorially, "it doesn't look any different to old Spit?"

"Right," said Syd.

Johnnie completed his circuit and walked back to his new Squadron Leaders.

"As far as the Hun's are concerned," he added, "we'll just be easy meat, as usual!"

"Uh, huh!" said Dan.

"Perfect!" said Johnnie. "Then they're in for a few nasty surprises, aren't they!"

"And this little baby has another neat little surprise too!" said Dan raising his hand. "If you're ever in trouble and you need to get out quick, just climb on up and as soon as you hit 19,000 feet, the supercharger kicks in and Boom! . . ." Dan made a fast sideways hand movement like a Karate chop, ". . . you're outa there! Ain't no one gonna catch you."

Johnnie turned to the fitter with intrigue.

"You must show me around this engine sometime!" he said.

"Yes, sir," said the fitter, "and what about the fuselage? Shall I ask the rigger to paint your initials on the sides?"

"Absolutely," said Johnnie. "J. E. J. please and the Wing Commander's pennant on the tail too."

"I shouldn't do that if I were you," said Scrine, "too conspicuous. And you'd be a handsome scalp for some young enemy pilot trying to make a name for himself."

Johnnie creased a menacing smile.

"Look, those Focke's have had us sneaking around and hiding for over a year now. Now, if this thing is as good as it's supposed to be then I want them to know we're there. And if they want to come up and fight, then fine. That's exactly what we intend to do."

"Have it your own way, Johnnie," said Scrine blandly. "You also need to choose a call sign. Here's the list of available ones."

Scrine handed the list to Johnnie and after a few seconds he had made his choice.

"Bit fancy aren't they? Ah, here we are 'Greycap' plain and simple."

Before Johnnie took his new Spitfire for a test flight, Bill McCord took him for some lunch. As they strolled around the perimeter track they passed another bunch of Canadian pilots.

"They all look so young, Bill!" said Johnnie with concern.

"They may look it but I can assure you Johnnie they can fly, really fly. And in battle they'll give you everything . . . "

Then Bill stopped and faced Johnnie directly.

" . . . but they all know what happened to their buddies at Dieppe and they're in no mood for bullshit. I've got to be honest with you Johnnie – they want a Canadian leader. If you want their trust you're going to have to earn it."

"So what you mean is, I'm on approval."

"I guess so!"

Back in Melton Mowbray the story of Johnnie's success was everywhere. In the butcher's shop, the post office and the pubs, everyone who knew him had something to say. Local pride soared and a fund to buy a new Spitfire was set up. In the front parlour of the house on Welby Road, Johnnie's father sat reading the newspaper. Johnnie's mother and brother Ross sat on each arm of the chair looking on. Together they read an article in the *Melton News*, headlined:

HE'S A WING COMMANDER NOW!

"No career has been followed with more interest by his fellow townsmen than that of 'Johnnie' Johnson. Everyone was delighted to hear of his rapid promotion and readers everywhere will join in our congratulations..."

Mr. Pullinger sat in the headmaster's office at Loughborough Grammar School and read a similar article in the *Daily Sketch*. When he had finished the article he folded the newspaper neatly and put it to one side of his desk top. From the stationery rack in front of him he flicked out a sheet of his own personal headed notepaper and began to write.

The nation had already seen the fighter ace from Dieppe on cinema screens around the country and further news was eagerly awaited. But at RAF Kenley the mood was not quite so cheerful.

Johnnie knew very little of the combat experience of his new pilots so he called all thirty-six of them together in the briefing room, but when he entered the room it was stiflingly hot.

"Sheesh!" he said, "we don't have central heating where I come from!"

He walked over to the radiator, turned it down and opened the window. Dan and Syd Bradford sat at the front of the unimpressed gathering. At the back of the room a handsome baby-faced pilot called Craig muttered under his breath.

"So come to Yellowknife. That'll freeze your ass!"

Friends around him struggled to suppress their sniggers as Johnnie walked up to the blackboard and started to draw the outlines of Spitfires on it.

"Great!" muttered Craig, "back to school!"

Despite his baby-faced looks, Craig had won the sword of honour during his RCAF training in Canada. He was a courageous fighter with a mischievous whit and was extremely popular with the other pilots.

"So," said Johnnie loudly, "how do you prefer to attack?"

Silence. Johnnie looked at Syd Bradford and pointed with the chalk.

"Squadron Leader? We'll start with you!"

"Well," Syd replied, "the Squadron Leader flies at the front and the rest follow in a line."

"And they all protect his arse, right?" said Johnnie in dismay.

"You got it!" answered Syd.

Johnnie pointed to the 'V' formation he had drawn on the blackboard.

"Has anyone flown like this?"

There were blank stares all around the room until Syd spoke again, "Nope!"

Johnnie held out his right hand with his fingers spread.

"Right then. Imagine each fingernail is a Spitfire and the leader is the middle finger."

Johnnie waved his hands around each other.

"We can move around freely. Each formation can attack and defend at will."

Craig grumbled to the pilot next to him under his breath.

"Abracadabra, hey presto we win!" he said in astonishment. "Can you believe this guy? Next thing you know he'll be teaching us nursery rhymes!"

"We like to fly in line!" said Syd loudly. "It's how we've been trained!"

It was clear that Bill McCord was right. There was no way Johnnie's new pilots were going to be won over with words. All he could do was conceal his annoyance and take up the challenge.

"Okay, Syd, we'll practice. Dan, you and I will fly our sections in the 'V' formation. Syd, you can fly inline – and we'll see how it goes."

The following day Johnnie, Dan and Syd each led a section of four Spitfires over the English Channel.

"Syd, you take your section, fly above me and replace Dan on my left side. Dan, you fly below me and replace Syd on my right. Ready? – Rotate!"

The two sections of Spitfires exchanged places but Syd's section snaked untidily. Johnnie watched and waited as Syd's section finally got into position.

"Okay Syd!" called Johnnie, "now make a V-formation."

Johnnie listened to the confused radio talk and waited again while Syd rearranged his Spitfires around himself.

"Right let's try it again," said Johnnie, "ready – rotate!"

Much to Syd's surprise the next exchange was executed

with neat precision.

"Any problems with that Syd?" asked Johnnie.

Before Syd could answer Dan made an urgent call and flicked the safety catch of his guns to 'armed'.

"Greycap! Large section of bandits inland, five miles, eleven o'clock."

All the other pilots looked over to the enemy fighters and then back at Johnnie in anticipation. Johnnie glanced around at the bandits.

"Greycap to all sections. Slow right turn on me."

All the pilots turned neatly in a huge graceful arc.

"Greycap to all sections. Blue leader you take the starboard bunch, Red Leader the port. Everyone select a target but stay in formation."

Johnnie watched and listened to the busy radio talk as the two sections quickly positioned themselves for attack.

"Greycap to all sections, turn to port. We're going home."

"JEEZ!" shouted Dan, "Goddamned Limey!"

Back at Kenley airfield the three sections of Spitfires came in to land one by one. Johnnie climbed down from his cockpit and acknowledged his riggers with a friendly nod and they set about their work. As he walked past the two other groups of pilots they stood in a quiet, sullen mood and turned to each other to light cigarettes.

"Officer's Mess!" shouted Johnnie. "Thirty minutes!"

In the Officers Mess lounge the eleven pilots slouched in their chairs murmuring. Johnnie entered the room, closed the door behind him and walked slowly and purposefully over to the fireplace. At first there was no reaction. Johnnie calmly and deliberately cast a steady gaze at each individual pilot. The murmuring stopped and one by one the pilots sat up straight in their chairs. When there was absolute silence Johnnie made his position clear.

"Who checked their fuel gauge?" demanded Johnnie angrily. "Anyone? There is no point in getting in a scrap if you haven't got the fuel to get home!"

Johnnie paused for a moment.

"You have all seen for yourselves how the V-formation works. But formation is not just about pretty patterns. Good formation is the only way we can look out for one another. Good formation can keep you alive. Dead pilots are no use to anyone!"

The cockiness of the pilots gave way to silent concentration.

"Right, then," said Johnnie. "That's the bollocking over! Now from what I have seen of today's performance I have to say your attack preparation is excellent. But you can forget all that stuff about defending the leader in the attack. Battles are fought, won or lost within minutes, seconds even. If we're going to start knocking the enemy down in large numbers there simply isn't the time for one man to make an attack while three others sit and wait to be attacked. From now on the leaders take you to the enemy and when we find them – we all attack together. We get in quick, hit them hard and get out quick. No heroics!"

The pilots looked around at one another with curiosity and caution. There were no smiles just frowns of concentration and suspicion.

"From now on," concluded Johnnie, "we change the way we fight."

Chapter Thirteen
BREAKTHROUGH

It was lunchtime in the Officer's Mess dining room and the atmosphere was quiet and subdued. Johnnie ate alone as the call came over the Tannoy.

"All Greycap units to come to readiness in one hour," Bill McCord announced.

Johnnie hurriedly finished his lunch, drained his teacup and got up to leave. The rest of the pilots sat and watched him in silence.

In McCord's office Johnnie was briefed on the raid which was to take place that afternoon.

"The Typhoon's will go in on a low level bombing run over the airfield at Abbeville," said Bill.

"And we take on any fighters that are stirred up," said Johnnie. "Sounds just like the Bader's last mission."

"Yes, pretty much so. Squadron Leader Clarke, codename 'Grass Seed', will coordinate the attack from Kenway radar."

Johnnie studied the map thoughtfully with uncomfortable reminders of Bader's disappearance.

"Well if we really want to take on these Fock Wulfs the only way is to ambush them," he said determinedly. "We don't really know what these Spit Nines can do in battle and so I want to make sure we've got complete surprise."

"You've got a good man in Clarke," said Bill, "he'll keep you out of the way until the time is right."

It was a fine spring day in early April and weather conditions were good as Johnnie led thirty-six Spitfires in V-formations of four high above the coast of northern France.

In the operations room Clarke sat above the plotting table as WAAFs used long plotting sticks to move markers around the huge map. Clarke was a debonair man with a calm demeanour and a sharp, analytical mind. He watched as the WAAFs moved the Typhoon markers in a turn for home. Other WAAFs moved Johnnie's markers closer towards them. Clarke picked up the phone and pressed the radio talk button.

"Greycap from Grass Seed. The Typhoons are on their way home. You should see them below you now."

Johnnie looked down and saw the Typhoons. In the distance were the columns of smoke from their attack of a few minutes earlier.

"Roger Grass Seed," Johnnie's reply was heard over the control room Tannoy, "I see them."

One of the WAAFs placed new markers on the map just a little further inland from Johnnie and Clarke called up again.

"Greycap from Grass Seed. Bandits. Estimate forty of them. Well below you at fifteen thousand. Steer port on three one zero. I'll bring you in from the sun."

Johnnie wheeled the entire wing on a tight, well-disciplined, left-hand turn and he spotted the bandits exactly where Clarke had predicted. Everything was going according to plan.

"Greycap to all units. Forty plus Huns below, three o'clock. Red Squadron you go port."

"Roger Greycap," said Dan.

"Green Squadron to starboard."

"Roger Greycap," said Syd.

"Blue Squadron follow me. Everyone select a target, keep formation and wait for the word."

The three Squadrons of twelve Spitfires each divided into three strict formations as they moved into position. In the operations room one of the WAAFs placed three new bandit markers on the map further inland over France.

"Greycap from Grass Seed," Clarke called. "Second strong formation of bandits behind you. Exercise caution."

Johnnie looked over his shoulder.

"How far, Grass Seed?"

"Hard to tell Greycap. The radar's at its limit. Could be one mile, could be ten."

Johnnie spotted the second formation of bandits. They were in the distance but closing rapidly on his tail.

"Greycap to all sections, attack formations."

Every section of four Spitfires fanned out like huge claws above the unsuspecting Focke Wulf 190s below. The entire wing of thirty-six Spitfires was evenly spread above the first enemy formation. The pilots all flicked their gun switches to armed, looked over at Johnnie and waited for the call.

It was tight. If Johnnie called the attack and it was not quick enough he ran the risk of being caught between two huge gangs of enemy fighters. If he called it off there was just about enough time to get out alive. Johnnie's eyes flicked rapidly down at the first section, back at the second section and around his men. With clear decisiveness he made his precisely timed call.

"Greycap to all sections. Get in now!"

In the operations room Clarke heard Johnnie's orders over

the Tannoy.

"I hope you know what you are doing Johnnie," he said to himself.

All the Spitfire pilots punched at the throttles and they all screamed down and sliced diagonally through the first bandit formation in one massive simultaneous attack. Scores of orange cannon and machine gun tracers streaked down from the wings of every Spitfire, filling every piece of sky above the enemy with lead. Two Focke Wulfs exploded immediately. In rapid succession four were hit, burst into flames and spiralled down pouring black smoke.

In the operations room Clarke had seen enough.

"Grass Seed to Greycap," he called urgently, "second formation of Bandits now on top. Withdraw. Repeat, withdraw!"

Johnnie looked up and behind to see the second attack being lead by the Focke Wulf 190 with the Ace of Clubs and Ace of Clubs logo. For a fleeting moment his instincts urged him to turn and counter attack. But he had men to bring home.

"All Greycap units. Do not form up. Climb to 19,000 and get out."

All thirty-six Spitfires pulled up in fast climbs until their superchargers kicked in, hurling them forwards with scorching acceleration. Even before the first section of the enemy fighters had time to think about a counter attack, Johnnie and his men were already gone. But in one long, frustrated look back, Johnnie watched the Ace of Clubs as it was left behind in the distance.

At Kenley airfield Johnnie, Syd and Dan stood by Johnnie's Spitfire, smoked cigarettes and waited for the last remaining pilots to return. Johnnie looked concerned and checked his watch. Syd scanned the horizon yet again.

"There's two now, sir," he said.

"That still leaves one missing," said Johnnie in subdued tone. "He'll be out of fuel by now. So he's either dead or at another airfield. Come on, let's go and find the rest of the boys."

Inside the dispersal hut the commotion was deafening. Euphoric pilots slapped backs, laughed and congratulated each other. One last pilot stood in front of Scrine who was trying to listen to his combat report above the noise. When Johnnie, Syd and Dan walked in, the hut fell silent.

"Six!" said Scrine," six Focke Wulfs were confirmed destroyed.

A huge cheer went up and the pilots crowded around Johnnie to congratulate him. For the first time ever a heavy loss had been inflicted on the Butcher Birds with only the unconfirmed loss of one pilot.

Air Vice Marshall Stevens' vision had become a reality, Johnnie's first Canadian Wing were ready and up for the fight.

In the Officer's Mess bar that night the excitement continued unabated. By that time Johnnie had heard most of the anecdotes from everyone except Syd, who kept a discreet distance. A very drunken Craig demonstrated his kill to Johnnie with the same hand-swooping movements that Johnnie had first demonstrated a couple of days earlier.

"... and then I came in next to Dan like this and Abracadabra, hey presto, I nailed him before he even knew I was even there!"

"No, Craig!" said Johnnie.

"Huh?"

"You don't wave your hands around like that. You have to tuck your thumbs under your palms first, like this. See?"

"Okay. Right, I got it!" said Craig.

Johnnie turned to the bar and waited to be served.

"If you don't mind me saying so, sir," said Dan, "that was a pretty damned good show up there today."

"Thank you, Dan," said Johnnie turning back.

"For a Limey, that is!" Dan joked.

"That's – 'Goddamned Limey, Sir!' to you."

"Excuse me, sir?"

"Just watch what you're saying with the radio talk switch on!"

Realising his earlier mistake when they were out on training, Dan was stuck for words.

"Buy me another beer and that'll be the end of it!" Johnnie grinned.

"Yes, sir!"

Much unspoken respect was developing between the two men. As far as Dan was concerned Johnnie put the team before his rank and had given every man equal purpose. As far as Johnnie was concerned, Dan was an American who had left the safety of his home and joined the Canadian Royal Air Force well before the USA had entered the war. And even later, when he had been offered more pay to fly with the USAAF, Dan had chosen to stay.

The following morning Johnnie was sitting at his desk in his office when there was a knock at the door.

"Come in!" called Johnnie.

Into the office walked Syd Bradford.

"Syd. Morning."

"Morning, sir," said Syd, uncharacteristically quiet.

Johnnie stopped writing and sat back in his chair as Syd approached.

"I've been talking with the other guys, sir . . ."

"Yes?"

" . . . and I've got to tell you, well . . . "

Syd paused, reached into his pocket and pulled out two small pieces of cloth. He laid them deliberately on the desk in front of Johnnie who looked down at them. The blue shoulder flashes had the word 'Canada' embroidered on them.

" . . . the boys would like you to wear these. After all we are Canadians and we've got to convert you."

"You do realise this is strictly against regulations?"

Syd simply grinned knowingly and nodded.

"Thanks, Syd. I'll get them sewn on today."

Chapter Fourteen
BURN OUT

The first successes against the Focke Wulf 190s marked a major breakthrough in the struggle for air superiority, and once again the RAF was able fight on equal terms. Having at last won their trust, Johnnie's new pilots rewarded him with absolute loyalty and friendship. The combination of his tactics and their airmanship resulted in a dramatic rise in the score of the Canadian wing and, as a result, in the late spring of 1943 Johnnie was called to Buckingham Palace to be awarded the Distinguished Service Order.

His train journey there took him past some of the suburbs of London which bore the brunt of nightly saturation bombing. Entire streets and hundreds of homes had been completely destroyed. Workmen picked through the piles of rubble brick by brick. Police lifted bodies into ambulances and parents loaded up prams with anything they could salvage – but where would they go next? In the air it was kill or be killed. A fighter stood a chance. But for civilians who were not fortunate enough to have their own Anderson shelter or live near a tube station, all they could do was sit under the dining table, hold onto one another and hope that the death whistles of the night sky were not directly above.

News of the success of the Canadian wing spread among pilots on both sides of the Channel and it was not long before Paula became the focus of media attention. Almost daily, gentlemen of the press would wait outside Norwich Fire Station where she worked. Always polite, even if a little chastened, she would patiently answer questions until inevitably Johnnie's least favourite would be asked.

"Do you think he will beat Sailor Malan's record, Paula?"

A short while after his visit to Buckingham Palace, Johnnie met with Bill McCord and Jamie Jameson in the planning room of Fighter Command at RAF Uxbridge. Two large maps hung on the wall each peppered with scores of little red dots. One map was labelled 'March 1943' and had large concentrations of dots over the Channel and southern England. The other map for 'June 1943' showed much fewer dots deep inland from the coast of northern Europe. Each dot represented activity of the Focke Wulf 190s as recorded by the RAF.

"As you can see," said Jamie, indicating on the maps, "the effect of the Spitfire Nine has been to clear the English Channel and push the bastards right back into Europe. This now provides a relatively safer daylight passage for the American Forts on their way to targets in Germany."

"But without long range tanks, we can't go all the way with them," said Johnnie.

"You don't have to. You take them as far as you can and then hand them over to the American fighters. They take them to Germany while you rearm and refuel. When they come back out of Germany you take over again."

It was yet another change for Johnnie and his men and he considered the likely scenarios carefully. From what he had seen of the American bombers he had been greatly impressed but he was still worried about the Focke Wulfs.

"They can be really unpredictable," he said. "They keep moving to different airfields and they have a nasty habit of popping up when you least expect them. What we really need is a rapid response outfit."

"Which is exactly what you're going to be!" said Jamie.

"How's that?" asked Johnnie.

"We're going to keep you on the move," Jamie explained. "When spies send us sightings of enemy fighters at airfields in Europe, we'll move you around our own temporary ones to get you nearer in readiness for attack. You'll live under canvas and be ready to switch at short notice."

So the travelling road show of the first Canadian 'Tactical Wing' was born, and with it the guarantee that Johnnie and his men would be kept well and truly in the Front Line.

On 17 August, one of the biggest bombing raids in history targeted the industrial heartland of Nazi Germany. A massive assembly of nearly two hundred US Flying Fortresses set off to attack the ball bearing factories at Schweinfurt and the Messerschmitt complex at Regensburg. But by the time Johnnie's escort wing reached Antwerp they had not seen a single enemy fighter. Being at the limit of their range they handed over to the American fighters and turned for home to refuel. As always the Flying Fortresses flew with great precision and as Johnnie watched the proud, orderly, box formations disappear on the horizon, he could only imagine what lay ahead of them.

Having refuelled, the Tactical Wing returned across the North Sea and headed for Holland. But it was a mournful sight which befell them. Still at 20,000 feet and still holding formation, the Flying Fortresses limped homeward having suffered a terrible mauling at the hands of the Focke Wulfs. Sixty less in number, the surviving aircraft were badly shot up and there were huge gaps in their formations. Undercarriage wheels hung down, burned out engines hung out of their cowlings and great holes gashed their wings and fuselages. Some of them, looking like weakling birds which could not keep up with the rest of the flock, straggled in pitiful isolation. But still the Butcher Birds had not finished with them.

Low on fuel and spent of ammunition, the American Mustang fighters had thrown everything they had at the Focke Wulfs. But like endless packs of hyenas picking at the wounded, they kept swooping in and gnawing at the bombers again and again. As the American fighters turned for Britain, Johnnie's men took over and the bomber pilots were given the renewed hope of a fresh, fully-armed escort.

Looking high to his right, Johnnie saw a large formation of enemy fighters splitting into three sections with the clear intention of picking off some isolated bombers. He immediately divided his wing into three squadrons and, with the extra speed of the super chargers, they wheeled in tight turns towards the predators.

To the Allies, the Flying Fortresses offered a lifeline, but to the Nazis they were a knife to the heart. The stakes could not have been higher and for Johnnie and his men it was air combat of the fiercest kind. Bitter close-run battles raged as the Spit Nines were flown to their limits in desperate struggles to keep the swarms of Butcher Birds off the American bombers.

Once clear of the coast of Holland, the Focke Wulfs were

eventually driven off and the Flying Fortresses were left only with the sight of friendly Spitfires with their distinctive elliptical wings forming around them and taking them home. To the American bomber crews, the sight of the RAF fighters was as welcome as their own and huge respect and trust was built between the two independent air forces. News of the collaboration soon spread and Johnnie and the Canadian Tactical Wing became household names on both sides of the Atlantic.

Jamie Jameson developed an uncanny knack of directing Johnnie to the enemy and nearly every day during the summer months of 1943, dog fights of ferocious intensity raged around the Flying Fortresses. As Stevens had predicted, the Canadian Tactical Wing racked up an impressive score and awards were made for landmark figures. When Johnnie shot down his twentieth enemy fighter it was the wings ninety-ninth, and to mark the occasion he was presented with a silver tankard.

But even in times of high spirits the brutal attrition of war took its insidious toll. Camaraderie could lift morale but there was no antidote to battle fatigue. For everyone, endurance had its limits.

It was during mission briefings that Bill McCord first began to notice the tell-tale signs in Johnnie. Unlike other pilots he had not developed an involuntary tick or 'The Twitch'. Instead he had lost weight, developed dark rings beneath his eyes and looked permanently tired. But it was his combat reports that gave rise to the greatest alarm.

On the 5 September 1943, the Canadian Tactical Wing

had received orders to escort yet more Flying Fortresses returning from a mission deep into France. The grim spectacle of so many crippled bombers struggling home had become an all too familiar sight, as were the swarms of Focke Wulfs which harried them. Unable to gain the advantage of surprise, Johnnie had had no choice but to lead his men into an immediate head-on attack. Pairs of opposing fighters twirled around one another as the Spitfires fought desperately to drive the enemy fighters away from the depleted bombers.

Johnnie found his range on a solitary Focke Wulf and was about to go in for the kill when he noticed that the Ace of Clubs had locked onto Craig, who was flying as call sign 'Blue Two'. Johnnie broke off and flew directly into the attack but he was unable to get there before Blue Two was sprayed with machine gun and cannon fire. Within seconds Craig's Spitfire was ablaze.

"Get out, Blue Two! Johnnie shouted. "For God's sake man, bale out!"

Craig struggled with his canopy as the cockpit filled with thick, black, choking smoke.

"I can't!" Craig coughed, "It's stuck. The canopy's stuck!"

Suddenly flames burst through the floor of the cockpit and advanced rapidly around Craig's feet in a roaring furnace.

In the Operations room at Kenway, Craig's desperate plight could be heard over the Tannoy.

"Get me out, get me out! Oh God, oh God. No! No!"

The WAAFs looked up at the tannoy in horror.

Craig pumped his legs frantically in a useless attempt to

escape the flames and his last desperate seconds were heard by all.

"Please! Get me out. I'm burning. Please . . "Oh God! No! Please . . ."

Johnnie flicked his radio talk switch and suddenly Blue Two's transmission was cut off.

In the Operations room the sickening screams were suddenly silenced and all that could be heard was the eerie crackle of static. One of the WAAFs took out a handkerchief and sobbed. High above the plotting table Clarke eased his collar uncomfortably.

Blue Two sliced silently into the sea without wreckage and within seconds the white splash was engulfed by blue heaving water. Distracted for a second, Johnnie had lost his angle on the Ace of Clubs which was turning back towards him. But with only enough fuel for his return to Britain, Johnnie was forced to turn away and he left his old adversary behind.

As soon as he completed his debrief and filed his combat report, Johnnie returned to his caravan to find Sally asleep on his bed. When he walked in she jumped up to greet him but he just pushed her gently to one side. He clumped off his flying boots, flopped onto his bed and fell asleep. But it was a restless and fitful sleep. His head and neck twitched, his eyelids flickered and his breathing became irregular.

Suddenly there was a rapid knock on the door like a machine gun. Startled and sweating Johnnie sat bolt upright and Bill McCord entered the caravan. Johnnie swung his legs round and sat on the edge of the bed. Bill sat on the chair next to Johnnie's desk.

"Johnnie, I've been reading your mission reports and your score is nearly forty."

"But many of those are unconfirmed," Johnnie answered suspiciously.

"And they're not good enough, are they?"

"Sir?"

"You're taking too many risks. You're going for the kill when you could be sending someone else in. It's just not like you Johnnie."

The two men observed one another for a few uncomfortable moments before Bill delivered the news.

"It's over, Johnnie. You're grounded. Hugh Godefroy takes over from you tomorrow. Make sure you're in mess tent tonight."

Bill left the caravan with the door slightly ajar. Johnnie pushed it open and the fragrant early evening air wafted in. He stretched his neck to look outside at the busy camp scene. Riggers and fitters worked on Spitfires, pilots walked and talked, smoke and steam billowed from out of the kitchen tent, fuel trucks and supply wagons passed by. He remembered the happy spirit of Bader's team and how he had struggled to get it back. But just like the time of Bader's capture within a heartbeat, it was gone again.

In the packed mess tent Air Vice-Marshall Stevens had made the journey especially to be there. Bill McCord quietened the celebrations and handed over to him.

"Johnnie," said Stevens, "I'll come straight to the point. All these Canadians gathered here . . ."

"And American!" shouted Dan from the back.

"All these Canadians – and American," Stevens continued, "have clubbed together and asked me to present you with this."

Stevens handed a small jewellery box to Johnnie. The tent was in absolute silence as he opened it. Inside was a beautiful gold watch.

"Good Lord!" he exclaimed.

Spontaneous applause erupted and Johnnie held the watch up for all to see. When the cheering finally subsided, he struggled to find words.

"Well!" he gasped, "I feel like I'm being retired from the firm!"

Laughter and further applause broke out as men gathered around to congratulate him. The inevitable party ensued and it was an evening of particular pride and satisfaction for Stevens who later took Johnnie to one side and filled his glass with a stiff gin.

"I never doubted you for a moment, Johnnie!"

"So all this was your idea then? The Canadian Wing, I mean."

"Well it took a little help from some others."

"I knew it couldn't have been AVM Davidson!"

"That's all behind you now," said Stevens reassuringly.

"And so it would seem, is this."

In the few uninterrupted minutes that Johnnie and Stevens could manage together, they shared amusing anecdotes but still Johnnie could not relax.

"So, sir?" he enquired, "once all the fun is over – when do I go back? To the Front, I mean."

"Well, right now you've got two whole weeks to spend with your beautiful wife. Lucky man!"

"And then?"

"You'll join Jamie Jameson in the mission planning office at Uxbridge. Interesting work, you'll enjoy it."

"And then?"

"That's it. It's over, Johnnie. You're not going back to the Front."

Chapter Fifteen
NEAR MISS

The news of Johnnie's return to Melton Mowbray was received by Paula with such sublime relief that she hardly dared believe it. The stories and photographs in the *Daily Sketch* had thrilled and lifted the hearts of the nation, but for her there had been a price of torment to pay.

Johnnie walked around the side of his parent's house and into the back garden like he had never been away. When Paula first saw him from the end of the garden she immediately recognised the broad upright frame of her husband but there was no hurry in his walk. His uniform was baggy and loose and his cheeks were sunken and grey. The smile was still there but his eyes were dull and lacklustre.

When they embraced his broad back was somehow harder and unyielding. He smelled different too. Not unwashed, but not clean. It was a sort of musty canvas smell of an old church hall curdled with aviation fuel and the tangy acetone of cordite. But worse, there was no passion, no urgent rush for the bed. Instead Johnnie was just happy to sit at the table next to the orchard and watch the wasps buzzing around the ripening apples. This was going to take time.

Whether he liked it or not Johnnie was a national celebrity and the local council had planned a busy schedule for him.

Like most towns and villages in Britain, Melton had organised a morale-boosting week of celebration to raise money for an

RAF Spitfire. The main event was a huge celebration parade. With much improvisation, shopkeepers, Scouts and Girl Guides had turned the marketplace into an area of lively civic celebration. A huge banner reading 'Wings for Victory Week' was stretched across the upstairs windows of several shops. Running through the middle of the banner was a tall savings thermometer with a model Spitfire half way up it. Bunting and Union Jacks hung everywhere and nearly every shop window displayed a large Victory 'V' sign. A large wooden stage had also been erected in the middle of the square on which Johnnie was to be part of a gathering of local dignitaries. At the very time when all Johnnie wanted was to be alone with Paula, a huge effort was being made to put him on display.

On the day of the parade, Johnnie dutifully sat on the stage with Paula and his family and they were all surrounded by a group of anonymous dignitaries. A lengthy procession marched by in which everyone was represented. The Army, Royal Navy, RAF, Home Guard, Police, WVRS, Land Army Girls, Scouts and Guides all filed by and Johnnie took their salute. Finally the end was marked with a horse and cart carrying scrap aluminium into which women threw old pots and pans, supposedly to be used to build aeroplanes. After the procession and gala celebrations, the stage was dismantled, the bunting was taken down and weary children were taken home. It was time for some tea and privacy.

When Johnnie returned home scores of his teenage fans were waiting for him. Pretty girls sat along the garden wall and when they saw his car they all rushed towards it. While Paula and his family went inside the house, Johnnie signed every autograph book and was smothered by admiring hugs and kisses. It was a complete surprise but it was all bloody good fun.

Unsurprisingly, Paula did not see it that way, and to make matters worse when Johnnie finally managed to tear himself away, there was another huge sack of fan mail waiting for him inside the house.

In the parlour Johnnie's mother served tea as Johnnie sifted through the pile of letters. Then one with a Loughborough Grammar School stamp caught his eye and he was just about to read it when Paula left the room and ran upstairs. Johnnie tucked the letter in his jacket pocket and followed her up.

"Paula!" he called.

Paula stopped at the top of the landing and faced him. Should she throw herself on the bed and cry? No. Never mind if he was a national hero, Johnnie was her man and this thing needed to be sorted. He approached with caution.

"What?" she demanded.

Unlike the vulnerable girl he had dragged into a gin palace in Blackpool, Johnnie was confronted by a woman who was proud, but wounded, and in no mood for compromise.

"Paula. Look, darling," Johnnie struggled and words were not enough. "Oh! Let's go out tomorrow."

Out on the root fields of Leicestershire Johnnie was reunited with his boyhood. It was the first time he had had the chance to introduce Paula to shooting and he hoped that in the future it would be a happy pastime for them both. But with her back turned and her fingers stuck in her ears, she cringed as Johnnie downed another partridge with a single shot. The bird thumped to the ground some twenty yards away and Sally ran off to retrieve it. Paula sneaked a horrified peep and then turned away again. When Sally returned with the limp animal in her mouth, Johnnie noticed that she was limping. As she dumped the bird at his feet Johnnie bent down to look at her paw.

"Hold this for me please, darling," and he offered his gun to Paula.

Looking very unsure, Paula took the gun with it pointing down near Johnnie's feet. Johnnie picked up Sally's injured paw.

"That's a nasty thorn, old girl. Here, we'll soon have it out."

Holding Sally's paw firmly, he nipped the thorn out cleanly. Sally let out a loud yelp which made Paula jump and she accidentally fired the remaining cartridge. The shot hit the earth just feet away from Johnnie spraying bits of earth and sugar beet all over him and Sally.

Paula shook with horror and surprise.

"Oh darling!" she gasped, "I'm sorry – so sorry. I just don't know how it happened."

"Here, let me take that for you," said Johnnie with a grin.

He took the shotgun, broke it and emptied the spent cartridges, but Paula still stood quivering with alarm.

"You know, that's closer than the Luftwaffe has ever got!" he said sardonically.

"Oh Johnnie, don't say that!"

"Why? Oh, Paula please, what is it? What's the matter?"

"You're never out of the newspapers! You get mobbed by

teenage girls! And now this! I mean what am I supposed to do?"

"Aim up a bit!"

Paula tried desperately not to laugh but she could not resist his boyish charm. Johnnie laid the shotgun down, put his arms around her and gave her a long, loving hug.

"Can't we go away somewhere?" she said with longing. "Somewhere where they don't know you, just the two of us?"

"Why not?" said Johnnie.

Chapter Sixteen
POISONED WORDS

During the interval of his show, Dave Morris paid his customary visit to the theatre lounge for a drink and a chat with some of the audience. After he edged his way through the crowded room he reached the bar where Johnnie and Paula were waiting to be served.

"Large whiskey?" Johnnie asked him over his shoulder.

Recognising the rich Leicestershire accent, Dave turned around and squinted at him through his thick glasses.

"Johnnie! Paula! Why didn't you tell me you were coming?"

"Bit of a last minute thing," said Paula.

As the three chatted, some of the women of the audience across the other side of the bar recognised Johnnie and whispered to one another, but this time there were no intrusions.

All too soon the theatre lounge started to empty for the second half of the show. Dave made his apologies, but before he left for the stage door he invited Johnnie for a round of golf. Johnnie hesitated.

"That's alright," said Paula mischievously, "I can go shopping."

Dave left them to finish their drinks and for the first time since the start of his leave, Johnnie no longer had that grey pallor in his cheeks. The etched lines on his forehead had softened and he held Paula's hand like he used to. Paula linked arms with him, gave his hand a squeeze and they made their way back into the theatre.

The following morning Johnnie and Dave boarded an empty double decker tramcar by North Pier and went upstairs to take in the views. Out of town and along the cliff tops, all that could be heard was the hum of an electric motor and the rumble of the wheels on the track. Once again Johnnie experienced the serenity of a place where the threat of war was suspended. The Luftwaffe passed over Blackpool regularly but only stray bombs ever fell. In bizarre contrast to the east end of London, all of the hotels and guest houses which lined the sea front were untouched. Little wonder so many servicemen spent their leave there.

At Blackpool North Shore Golf Club the two men walked out of the club house, around the flag staff and fountain and onto the first tee. Dave nodded in the direction of Blackpool Tower in the distance.

"They'll never bomb that thing you know!" he said. "The Luftwaffe navigate by it. I've watched them. They turn left for Belfast, right for Sheffield or carry straight on for Glasgow."

Out on the open golf course all that could be heard was the call of seagulls and the swish and click of club and ball. Away from the pressure cooker of the Front Line Johnnie was quite happy for someone else to lead the conversation. Dave saw humour in just about everything. As an infantryman in the First World War he had survived its horrific slaughter and was nearly blinded by a gas attack in the trenches. But his anecdotes of those times still had a comedic twist. Ever since their first encounter in Blackpool Tower Ballroom, Johnnie had warmed to him, and out on the fairways they shared their earlier experiences.

"So those glasses you wear," asked Johnnie, "they're not part of your stage act then?"

"Nope. I can't see a thing without them!" Dave sniggered.

"Oh, I am sorry," said Johnnie.

"Don't be," said Dave. "I was one of the lucky ones. Anyway tell me about this girl in the swimming pool?"

"Oh, yes!" said Johnnie. "Well she was only the daughter of some Lord or something. Old Pullinger hit the roof when he found out."

"So what happened then?"

"She went on to Oxford. I had to leave school without a reference and that's why I failed my first RAF interview – and second."

"Sounds about right!" said Dave, sagely.

Half of the holes of the golf club had been given over to the 'Dig for Victory' effort and so after a detour around the root crops, sheep and chickens, the two men finished on the eighteenth and went back into the clubhouse. Out on the balcony overlooking the course they drank beer and surveyed the hills of the Lake District and Pennines.

"So once your leave is over, what then?" asked Dave.

"Well you know I can't tell you, but you can bet it'll be a desk job."

"With a girl like Paula to come home to, is that such a bad thing?"

"Go on tell me how lucky I am," Johnnie sighed.

"Well, you are."

"I know," said Johnnie, "but I don't think you understand, it's the flying, it gets in the blood. It's a way of living."

"And dying!"

"That's a risk we all take. I need to get back."

Dave raised his left arm and squinted hard at his watch.

"It's nearly time for my matinee performance," he said. "Come on, we'll have to drink up and go."

They retraced their steps to the promenade and sat in the tram shelter opposite the Miner's Home. All around them scores of servicemen strolled with their wives and girlfriends. Johnnie just gazed out to sea. Dave tried to read his face through his thick glasses but in the low September sun it was too bright for him. They rested their heads back on the edge of the bench, closed their eyes and let the warm glow soothe their faces.

"But what if you go away and don't come back?" asked Dave.

"I might not."

Deeply disturbed, Dave sat up and turned to face Johnnie.

"And leave Paula with no children?" he said. "Look at me Johnnie. I'm a bachelor, and yes alright I'm lucky, I've got a bob or two, but every night I go home to an empty house. You need to think about that."

Johnnie kept his eyes closed and said nothing.

"Think about the future," Dave implored. "With or without you, think about the future for Paula."

The air was still and balmy and the sun was warm on Johnnie's face. Below, the sea could just be heard as it slapped lazily against the sea wall. Johnnie knew from the other pilots he had seen with battle fatigue that once they were grounded, they stayed grounded. After all, Dave did have a point. Perhaps he was trying too hard.

The tram taking them back to the North Pier was crowded with evacuated children wearing name tags on their lapels and with gas masks in cardboard boxes slung with string around their shoulders. Some looked excited as if on an adventure holiday others looked timid and exhausted. Sitting clutching their bags and suitcases they were watched over by a strict looking old lady standing nearby. Next to the stairs was a mother with a baby in a pram. Johnnie and Dave had to excuse themselves as they squeezed on board. Dave stowed his golf clubs under the stairs and they both stood next to the strict looking old lady and reflected on the morning's round.

"You can sometimes get away with an iron for the first three holes," advised Dave, "but you really need to use a decent wood. I mean the way you sliced off the second tee!"

"I didn't slice it. The wind caught it!"

"What wind?"

The tram stopped at Gynn Square and the old lady herded the children towards the exit as the folding doors opened.

"Right children," she said in a loud matronly voice, "when you get off, stand by the tram stop and don't move. Paul! Sue! You count them, there should be eleven."

Expecting the old lady to be the last to get off the tram, the conductor held the door in readiness.

"Just a minute!" she snapped and turned to look Johnnie straight in the face.

"Golf!" she snarled. "Can't you two men find anything better to do when there's a war on?"

Chapter Seventeen
THE UNKNOWN

In the planning room at RAF Uxbridge, Johnnie stood next to the planning table with Jamie. He had not seen the New Zealander since Dieppe and after a brief catch up, Jamie spread a large map out in front of them. Johnnie rested his hands on it.

"So this is where all the ideas come from?" he asked.

"Well Churchill and Eisenhower have the ideas. All we have to do is make them work."

"That could take all night."

"It nearly always does!" said Jamie. "Most of the raids involve linking up with the Americans to escort the Flying Fortresses."

But as on so many previous occasions there were yet more challenges ahead. The walls of the room were covered with scores of aerial photographs of strange concrete bunkers taken along the coast of northern France.

"They're too far inland for coastal defence," said Jamie. "The French Resistance are trying to find out what's in them but in the meantime High Command want them taking out."

"Bit hard to hit with heavy bombers aren't they, Jamie?"

"Quite, and fighters are no use against reinforced concrete. That's why so many Spitfire pilots are being recruited onto fighter-bombers."

"Typhoons?"

"They're the future! Even a Spitfire can carry a couple of five hundred pound bombs."

"The Spitfire is a fighter," Johnnie protested, "not a bloody cart horse!"

"You're just an old romantic, Johnnie. Look, small, fast, hard-hitting, precision ground attacks. That's what we're going to be planning, so you'd better get used to them."

The mere mention of 'ground attacks' reminded Johnnie of Rhubarbs the time he had nearly collided with Hugh over France.

"So what about Rhubarbs," he asked, "they're not exactly 'precision' are they? I'd ban them."

"Would you tell that to command?" asked Jamie.

"Damned right I would!"

In Air Vice-Marshall Stevens' office the atmosphere was very different from Johnnie's earlier encounters with Davidson, and he listened to Johnnie's case very carefully. High death rates among pilots, high risk to civilians and very little achieved. Stevens did not take too much convincing and agreed to 'look into it'. But there was something else on Johnnie's mind and he seized upon the moment.

"I'd like to request a posting back to the Front, sir. As soon as possible."

"Any particular wing?"asked Stevens.

"Yes. It has to be Canadian."

"And I suppose you would want Spit Nines?"

"Absolutely, sir."

"Nice try, Johnnie. But you are needed here."

In the Prime minister's war bunker Scrine delivered the latest in a number of disturbing intelligence briefings to Churchill and Eisenhower. Copies of the same photographs of the concrete bunkers in northern France lay on the large conference table. News of destruction of the heavy water production at Vemork in Nazi-occupied Norway had been welcome, but the Nazi nuclear weapons scientists escaped.

"Then we must assume that they are ahead of our own 'Manhattan Project'," conceded Eisenhower grimly.

"We certainly believe they are well on their way," Scrine explained, "but just how close are they to building an atomic bomb? So far we don't have that information. But let me show you something else."

Scrine turned off the lights and switched on the cinema projector. In the darkened room the three men watched an old 'Movietone Newsreel' film of a German experimental 'Flying Triangle' and listened to the original narration . . .

"*A German airman is trying out his novel machine at Cologne . . .*"

"Now this film was seen in cinemas all around Britain in 1935, and so there's no secret here," said Scrine.

The film narrator continued:

" *. . . it is in effect a pair of rigid wings without body or tail . . . this machine flies under its own power if necessary. . .* "

The film concluded with the slim profile of the 'bat wing' almost disappearing on the horizon before making a faultless landing.

Scrine switched the lights back on.

"What's so special about it?" asked Eisenhower.

"It's thin," explained Scrine, "and if it were to be made out of anything other than metal it would be virtually impossible to pick up on radar. Now we are only months away from our first jet fighter and the Nazis will almost certainly have jet engines of their own. If they were to put them in something like this, our scientists predict air speeds of anything up to 800 miles per hour. And the shape of its wings could give it a huge fuel capacity. It would in effect be a 'stealth fighter'. . ."

". . . Or bomber!" added Churchill.

"Quite!" said Scrine. "And, if the Nazis do have an atomic bomb, this thing might even be able to take it to New York."

"You're not serious!" exclaimed Eisenhower in astonishment. "How can you be sure about all of this."

"We can't!" said Scrine.

"There is only one thing more sinister than the threat of what we know," Churchill observed grimly, "and that is the threat of what we don't know."

"And whatever else Hitler is up to he is keeping it all well concealed," added Scrine. "Possibly in underground chambers."

Eisenhower rose to his feet and slipped on his raincoat.

"Prime Minister," he began, "war it seems is moving into a whole new dimension. The only way we can be sure of protecting ourselves against these threats is to completely overrun Germany by our ground forces – and as soon as possible! The invasion of Europe must go ahead at the earliest opportunity. I will arrange to meet with President Roosevelt tonight."

During the winter months of 1943 all manner of excavations and concrete bunkers were spotted springing up in the woods all around northern France. Night after night Johnnie peered through stereoscopic binoculars at endless aerial reconnaissance photographs which had been passed to him by Photographic Interpreters at RAF Medmenham in Buckinghamshire. In his new nocturnal burrow he became quite accomplished at matching the ground attacks of fighter bombers to any new targets as they emerged.

However, without the smell of the cockpit and the target in his sights he feared that mission planning was becoming all too much like a game. His repeated requests for a return to the Front were refused and with growing anticipation of the invasion of Europe, he decided it was time for a new approach to the High Command.

It was daybreak in the early spring of 1944 when Johnnie walked from the planning building to the operations block. Under his arm was a bundle of papers with details of that day's raids. Inside the operations building he walked down the stairs and into the large underground room. With the look of a bored civil servant he handed the plans over to the duty officer.

"Thanks Johnnie," said the duty officer and he handed Johnnie an envelope.

Johnnie waited until he had left the building before he opened it. In the clear, crisp, morning sunshine he read the memo from Fighter Command.

Once again Johnnie stood in Stevens' office knowing that filing a formal request for transfer was unlikely to be well received. As a mark of the officialdom, Stevens had made sure he had Johnnie's original RAF file in front of him. He opened by congratulating him on the successes of his planning and pointed out that it could only have been achieved by 'experience'. This time Johnnie was ready for him.

"Thank you, sir. But when we go over to Europe we don't know what we will find. We'll certainly face new problems and solving those too will take – experience!"

"You just don't give up do you, Johnnie? Sit down."

Both men were right, but there could only be one outcome. Stevens certainly had to choose a seasoned leader to go to France and he had already pondered over the choice for several weeks.

"Johnnie – when I took you off ops you were empty, exhausted. I've seen it before. The more burned out a pilot gets the more angry he becomes. All he can think about are the men he has seen killed."

This was it. Johnnie was being let down gently again. But this time Stevens continued.

"I've got to be sure you're ready. You've always looked after your men, Johnnie. I need to know you are going to look after yourself."

"Really I'm fine, sir."

"Bader said something like that – and now he's a prisoner of war."

"Sir, I was there when Bader went missing. Just after he went into the attack we were bounced. We were heavily outnumbered and had to break – but he just kept going. It's a lesson I'll never forget... Sir! I know how to look after myself!"

Stevens gave the matter a few more moments of careful consideration.

"Very well," he said, "you can take charge of the Canadian Wing at Tangmere. Some of the men you already know, others will be new to you. Your guess about the invasion date is as good as mine, but when it happens your wing will be the first to be based over there.

Stevens took a rubber stamp, inked it and then pressed it hard onto Johnnie's file. When he lifted it away the word Johnnie had waited for so long to see was clearly visible – OPERATIONAL.

Chapter Eighteen
OVERLORD

Outside the Whipper Inn in Oakham, Johnnie waited nervously. He checked his new gold watch and straightened his jacket. Passers-by gave the odd admiring smile at the distinguished Wing Leader and Johnnie smiled back coyly. When he heard footsteps behind him, Johnnie turned around to see Paula approaching. For a few awkward moments they just looked at one another. Paula attempted a smile but her lips quivered too much and her eyes grew sore with tears. She had never wanted him to see her like that. As he moved towards her she flung her arms around his neck and clawed at the back of his collar. She had always known he would go back and would never try to stop him. No one could have been any more proud of her man than she was, but not even her pride could dull the pain.

5 June 1944

Johnnie cleared the security barrier at Tangmere, drove his Lagonda up to the familiar old Officer's Mess and parked outside. As if sensing the occasion, Sally followed excitedly as he walked briskly into a hive of activity. Everywhere there were teams of pilots and ground crews making hasty preparations. Riggers carried belts of machine gun rounds around their necks while others loaded them up into the wings of Spitfires. Fuel wagons and jeeps passed by. Supplies were delivered into storage huts. Transport trucks arrived and men jumped out of the back carrying kit bags.

Dan checked an inventory with the good looking, dark-haired, French Canadian Squadron Leader, Larry Deschamps. Johnnie had made Larry's acquaintance two years earlier but he had not seen him since he had been shot down shortly after Bader's capture. As soon as they spotted Johnnie, Dan and Larry caught up with him.

"Good to have you back, Johnnie," said Dan. "You know it's on then?"

"Yes, when did you hear?" asked Johnnie.

"Bill McCord announced it about an hour ago, sir," said Larry. "Have you heard from Stevens?"

"Yes he confirmed ten minutes ago. Who have you brought with you, Larry?"

"Squadron Leader Rafe Deering," said Larry. "He's er, briefing his men now."

In the busy dispersal hut young Canadian pilots unloaded kit bags and pinned up posters of Canadian sweethearts. Magazines were strewn everywhere, the air was thick with cigarette smoke and the busy banter was deafening. Rafe, oblivious to the racket going on around him, was engaged in a heated game of craps in the middle of the floor. A pilot's hat bulged with money and Rafe rolled the dice again. Looking much younger than his twenty-two years, Rafe was a handsome, blond, bush pilot and the son of a gold-prospector who had made his way to Montreal to enlist with the RCAF. Even for a gifted pilot he had risen to rank of Squadron Leader in record time, but he still had the quick wit of a young rogue pioneer and a keen eye for opportunity.

When Johnnie walked in with Dan and Larry very little

attention was paid until one or two pilots started nudging each other and standing up. But, face down and intent on cleaning up the winner's pot, Rafe was too busy to notice his new Wing Commander.

"Come on," he shouted on his own, "let's go!"

Then the silence slowly dawned on him and he looked up.

"Jesus!" he said to himself.

When Rafe came to his feet and looked up, Johnnie was struck by an eerie discomfort. He could have easily passed for the young Craig who had burned to death nearly a year earlier.

"Sir!" said Rafe with a snappy salute.

As he looked around the eager young faces, Johnnie allowed himself a wry grin. Back among the chaos of the buccaneering Canadians he knew he was at home once more.

Few of them slept that night. The Normandy landing was to be the biggest amphibious assault in history and the air battle to protect it was expected to be 'The Big Show'. In the dormitories, farewell letters to loved ones, which it was hoped would never be posted, were written before a restless night in the bunk beds. Outside the riggers worked into the night making final preparations. In the distance the morbid drone of heavy bombers could be heard as they made their way towards the coastal defences of northern France on preparatory raids.

Tuesday 6 June 1944. D-Day

The three squadrons of Johnnie's wing were called to readiness well before daybreak. After breakfast they climbed aboard their Spitfires and started their engines. All around the field bright blue flames coughed from exhausts in the half light, and the throaty roar of thirty-six Merlin engines bellowed in chorus.

After taking off in sections of four, they formed up together over the southern coast of England and Johnnie set course for 'Sword' and 'Juno' beaches where the British and Canadian troops were already wading ashore. Almost sick with tension, pilots scanned the skies over choppy seas in search of the Luftwaffe. Below, the English Channel was crowded with naval ships of all sizes and scores of landing craft shuttled Allied troops who then waded ashore. The heavy guns of Royal Navy ships pounded Nazi coastal positions. Fire flashed from the mouths of German concrete pill boxes as their machine guns raked back and forth across the beaches.

But in the air the greatest risk was from that of collision with other Allied aeroplanes. Nervous eyes darted everywhere as each pilot waited for calls of enemy sightings. Johnnie's wing had been sent to relieve an earlier patrol which, although getting low on fuel, was still fully armed.

"Greycap to Green Leader," called Johnnie. "We can relieve your section now. Any sign of the Hun?"

"Sorry. Not a bloody thing!" was the disappointed reply. "There's plenty of flak inland and you'd better look out for the navy shelling too. But that's it!"

Johnnie's wing exchanged with Green section and patrolled westwards until they could see the American landing beaches of Utah and Omaha. Although it was difficult to see from a distance, it looked like the troops on Omaha beach were pinned down and taking heavy losses. The beach was strewn with dead bodies and even more washed around in the bloody red surf like driftwood.

"Greycap to all sections. Anyone see anything?"

"Plenty of Yanks . . . some Poles and Czechs . . . the only buggers who aren't here are the Germans!"

At the end of their patrol, Johnnie's wing returned home without firing a shot.

In the Mess dining room at Tangmere that night the disappointment was almost palpable. Before they ate, Johnnie looked around the frustrated unshaven faces and attempted a brief pep talk. But he knew the Canadians better than that and so he concluded with the promise of future battles.

"Look, once we get camped over there," he said, "we won't have to keep crossing over the Channel and so we can go looking further inland for them. I promise you, we'll find the bastards alright!"

Two days later he led his wing into land at the airstrip at St. Croix du Mer.

On the ground Johnnie familiarised himself with his new surroundings and chose an orchard as good cover for the airfield camp. Supply trucks had already started arriving and once the kitchens, workshops and billet tents were in position he took a stroll over to the nearby country lane. It was blocked with a continuous nose-to-tail, one-way procession of supply trucks, armoured vehicles and marching troops.

Over the next few days the Spitfire base became more established, but there was still no sign of the enemy fighters. Late one afternoon Group Captain Bill McCord arrived with a case of wine which had been gifted to him by some of the welcoming locals. That evening he sat and drank with Johnnie and Dan in a briefing tent. A wooden supply box with a single candle made a makeshift table and Bill poured the wine into enamel mugs.

"All the talk at Biggin Hill is about you and Sailor Malan's record," said Bill.

It was that question again.

"I'm not really too interested to be honest Bill," said Johnnie. "No point in having aces if we don't win the war. What I want to know is, where's the Hun? These lads have travelled halfway across the world for the biggest air battle in history and the opposition have cried off!"

"They've heard you're here!"

"I'm serious, Bill."

"So am I. You and your crazy Canadians . . . "

"And American!" said Dan.

". . . yes," Bill continued, "they just don't want to know anymore. Hitler's sent all his fighters over to the Russian Front."

"But, they can't all be over there?" insisted Johnnie.

"The real problem," said Bill, "is that Kenway radar is at its limits here and wherever the enemy fighters are, they're out of range. But we're setting up a new communication system and pretty soon we'll start to get sightings from our ground troops, and there's always the French Resistance of course. If you can just sit tight for a few days, we'll get you to them."

A temporary field control tent was set up and every conceivable method of information gathering was brought together in it for cross checking. Maps and lists of sightings of enemy movements were pinned up on a large board for analysis. Operations officers pored over evidence like detectives investigating a crime scene. The all-important radio operator sat in the relative safety of a deep dugout in the centre of the tent, and hour after hour he strained his ears in his headphones to eavesdrop on every hint of enemy activity.

For days Johnnie and his men stayed at readiness, and during their wait they would sit in their Spitfires and laze away the hours in the warm sun. Just a few miles away the war on the ground continued as the Allies tried to break out of Normandy, but they were being held back by the crack troops of the Nazi SS Seventh army. One afternoon Johnnie sat in his cockpit and studied some maps. Nearby, Larry chewed gum and read a French magazine while Rafe chatted with a rigger. Further away Dan listened to gramophone records as he checked his Spitfire's rudder and tail movements. In the background the constant crump of shelling could be heard. Somewhere bitter ground battles were being fought and yet sitting next to the shade of the orchard, all was peaceful.

"Sir! Sir!" A sudden shout came from the direction of the operations tent and the sergeant ran out and over towards Johnnie's Spitfire. Johnnie sat upright as he approached.

"Sir! Sir!" he panted. "We've found them! In the south. Loads of them! Here, look!"

Chapter Nineteen
WEAPONS OF MASS DESTRUCTION

On 12 June 1944, the first of the new generation of Nazi 'terror weapons' was unleashed on civilians. Originally intended to be launched from concrete ramps around Pas de Calais, high explosive V1 flying bombs or 'Doodle Bugs' were fired from mobile units around northern Europe and dropped indiscriminately on London.

In Churchill's bunker the news only confirmed the speculations of previous meetings.

"Hitlers obviously mass producing jet engines," said Scrine. "But this might only be the start. We've also known for quite some time that his scientists are working on a rocket."

"The V2? But their manufacturing bases at Peenemunde were bombed and destroyed last year," said Churchill.

"And now we're in Normandy we've captured their concrete silos," added Eisenhower.

Scrine stood up and pointed to a large map of Europe on the wall.

"Well, they're still building them somewhere. We've just had confirmed reports that last month a test rocket was fired from Blizna in southern Poland, here. It landed in the swamps of the River Bug near the village of Sarnaki, here, and it was captured by Polish Resistance. It's on its way back to Britain with a cinema film of it as we speak. But take a look at this."

Scrine produced a photograph of a V2 rocket on the back of a large transport truck.

"Our guess," he continued, "is that once these things are operational they will be moved around and fired at will from within anywhere in Nazi-occupied Europe. These things fly vertically up into the stratosphere and then drop onto their targets at well over the speed of sound. There will be absolutely no detection of launch and no advanced warning."

"Rockets! Stealth bombers! Atomic bombs! What else is he hiding?" declared Eisenhower angrily. "This war will not be over until we've searched in every Nazi forest, tunnel and back yard. We must get into Germany and soon!"

Scrine pointed at the map of northern France and continued his brief.

"All intelligence reports confirm that Allied ground forces are being prevented from breaking out of Normandy by the German Seventh Army – here."

"Then I take it we're agreed on our strategy for dealing with them?" said Churchill.

"Hell yes!" said Eisenhower. "We can't pussyfoot around any longer. If they won't retreat – we take them out!"

Throughout June and July of 1944, Hitler diverted fighters to cover the German Seventh Army which had been ordered to keep Allied ground troops pinned back. But this brought them into the range of Johnnie's men and spies on the ground were becoming more skilled at working in close cooperation with American Thunderbolts and Mustangs. No longer the rulers of the skies, even the Focke Wulfs began to suffer devastatingly heavy losses. Impressive score sheets were recorded and crates of champagne were wagered between squadrons who competed for the highest ones.

Morale soared.

But the success of Johnnie and his men attracted the attention of the German fighter ace, Walter Matoni who always flew in a distinctive long-nosed Focke Wolfe 190. Johnnie and Matoni soon became aware of each other's aircraft markings, but Matoni was a tricky and elusive opponent who would never engage in a fight unless all the odds were completely in his favour. With typically Canadian mischievous wit, Johnnie's pilots often tried to provoke him over the airwaves with rude and demeaning comments in the hope that eavesdropping Nazi radio operators would pick them up.

Inevitably the story found its way into the British press and from her parent's home in Norwich Paula read an embellished account in a copy of the *Daily Sketch*.

"RAF Spitfire Ace issues challenge to Matoni ... Wing Commander 'Johnnie' Johnson has written to the German fighter ace, Walter Matoni, challenging him to a 'duel in the sky'..."

On 17 August, after Johnnie returned from the second mission of the day, he handed his Spitfire over to his ground crew for servicing and made his way over to the debriefing tent. After he had filed his combat report, a sergeant from the British Forces Post Office brought him a letter with Paula's handwriting on the envelope. Back in his tent he dumped his flying gear, sat down on his camp bed, and began to read.

Dear Johnnie,
I went to see the Doctor today and he told me that
everything looks fine . . . but now I read in the papers that
you have written a letter trying to pick a fight with some
chap called 'Matoni' . . . Please tell me it is not true, darling.
You take enough risks already . . . and so by the time I see
you again you might already be a Daddy.
Take care of yourself.
All my love,
Paula

Suddenly Johnnie was snapped out of his dream of home by
the sound of an approaching car. Outside his tent Bill McCord
arrived in a jeep which was driven by an Army Sergeant.

"You'd better get in, Johnnie," said Bill, "Sorry! No time for
questions."

Johnnie tucked the letter into his breast pocket, climbed
in behind McCord, and the jeep sped away. They drove
for well over an hour before they finally reached a small,
unimpressive, but secluded stone-walled barn. It was
surrounded by a heavily-armed guard of infantrymen and
several inconspicuous 'civilian' Citroens were parked nearby.
By the doorway a small generator droned.

Inside the barn, the window shutters had been closed and
it was dimly-lit by improvised electric lamps. Hooks and other
farm implements hung from the thick wooden beams and the
place smelled strongly of cow dung. At one end of the barn a

large white sheet had been stretched over a map board. Ten RAF commanders were in attendance and they sat on barrels, straw bales, wooden boxes and whatever else they could find. Beside the white sheet Scrine waited with Army Colonel Jackson. Johnnie and Bill squeezed in among the men and a guard closed the door. The lights were switched off. After a few seconds of darkness, images flickered onto the white sheet to the accompaniment of the whirr of the projector at the back of the barn. Scrine wasted no time in delivering his address.

"What you are about to be shown has never been seen by any other commander in the field. Only the Supreme Allied High Command know of its existence."

The silent black and white film flickered. A V2 rocket was shown standing on a launch pad and immediately there was an uneasy murmur around the barn. The engine of the V2 fired and it began to rise.

"The V2 ballistic rocket," announced Scrine. "Hitler calls it his 'Wonder Weapon'."

The rocket climbed to two hundred feet, thrashed around out of control, and then crashed in a spectacular ball of flame. Relieved laughter rippled around the barn.

"And he might just be right," continued Scrine.

The laughter was quickly subdued as the next sequence was played. It showed another V2 rocket taking off smoothly and successfully. It climbed up high until its flame eventually disappeared into the clouds.

"We think some of the concrete bunkers around the Pas de Calais might have been intended to house these rockets. But most of those have been bombed and destroyed and the rest are currently in Allied hands."

Johnnie was numbed by a sense of revelation. Never, during all of those winter months of mission planning at Uxbridge, could he have imagined the enormity of his task.

The next film showed another V2 rocket being carried by a large transport truck.

"But now Hitler has highly mobile transport trucks. Very soon he will be able to launch these rockets from anywhere within Nazi-occupied Europe and within a very short set-up time. Now, consider this next scenario."

On the screen a map of Germany and surrounding countries was shown with diagrammatic illustrations of many launch sites and long-range targets.

"V2 rockets carrying high explosives could very soon be dropped all around Europe – and possibly beyond. And our guess is that he has the capacity to build thousands of them."

The lights were switched on and Scrine gave way as Colonel Jackson stepped forward. He removed the white sheet to reveal a large map of northern France and Germany.

"The simple truth is that if we don't find them soon, we could face annihilation in, who knows? Months? Weeks? Our only chance of preventing this is to overrun Germany with ground troops and search for them everywhere."

Jackson indicated on the map a huge red Nazi enclosure in northern France which was almost completely surrounded by green Allied forces. The only escape route was a narrow gap between the two towns of Falaise and Argenten. The Colonel jabbed a crayon at the enclosure.

"But we can't break into Germany because of this. Packed in

here are fifty thousand crack SS troops of the German Seventh Army. Hitler has ordered them to stay and hold us off in order to buy time to get his V2 rockets fully operational. Now! These men are fanatics of the toughest kind. We cannot force their surrender and we cannot take prisoners, our own supplies are stretched to their limits as they are. Hitler has left us with no other choice . . . They have to be destroyed . . . But the scale of the task will require more than Army field artillery. Bill . . ."

Jackson gave way to Bill McCord who stepped up to the map and, with a crayon, he divided the area of the Nazi enclosure into squares.

"Using an organised system of sectors, ground attacks will be divided between American, British and Canadian air forces."

As he spoke, Bill shaded in one small area of the pocket after another.

"As each sector is destroyed we move onto the next," he continued, "and we work our way all the way to the River Seine."

Once the map was completely shaded in Bill folded it back to reveal a reconnaissance photograph. SS troops, tanks and armoured cars were shown packed in like a huge traffic jam along a French country lane. He indicated to each end of the lane.

"This is how we begin each sector. First, each end of every lane will be bombed to prevent passage and escape. Then Typhoons go in with rockets to destroy tanks and armoured cars. Fighters will then follow them in and finish off the troops with machine guns and cannons . . ."

Bill swept his hand repeatedly over the length of the lane.

" . . . we strafe again and again until nothing moves down there. Then we move onto the next sector."

Back at the Spitfire camp the following evening, Johnnie relayed the mission details to his men in the briefing tent as the smell of cooked bully beef drifted around the orchard. The pilots sat in uncomfortable silence. Sensing the mood, Johnnie quoted the SS Army pledge to their leader.

" . . . *'Ich schwöre bei Gott'* . . . Do you know what that means?" he asked, "It means . . . 'I swear by God' . . . These men have sworn to God that they are prepared to die for Hitler. There is nothing they will not do for him. They have already killed thousands of our boys on the ground and if we let them escape they will be back to do the same again. Now I don't like this kind of work anymore than you do . . . but we have no choice."

Chapter Twenty
DANTE'S INFERNO

Just before dawn on the morning of 19 August 1944, Johnnie's men walked around and inspected their Spitfires in preparation for the day's work. The usual cine cameras were in place next to the cannons, the radio hatches were secured and the machine gun ports were covered with canvas and sealed with fresh resin.

Johnnie settled into his cockpit and was welcomed by the smell of varnish, high-octane fuel and engine oil. The familiarities of imminent battle were somehow reassuring. The Riggers helped him tighten his harness over his shoulders before making the final checks.

GUNSIGHT LIGHTS	ON
CANOPY	OPEN
FUEL MIXTURE	RICH

Then the Duty Officer fired the Very Gun by the radio tent at the edge of the orchard and a bright red Roman candle soared against the early sunrise. The mission was on.

The Rigger lifted the flap on the engine cowling and plugged in the electric cable from the ground accumulator.

FUEL COCK	ON
STARTER AND BOOSTER COIL BUTTONS	UNCOVERED

THROTTLE	OPEN (HALF AN INCH)
IGNITION SWITCHES	ON

With Johnnie's index and forefingers pressed on the starter and booster coil buttons, the propeller began to turn.

CONTACT

The propeller flicked into a blur as the base tone of the huge Merlin engine growled into life.

MAGNETOS	LIVE
OIL PRESSURE	RISING

Ready to go.

The red sky of daybreak brightened to pale blue over the troops of the Nazi SS Seventh Army. If they had dared to venture onto the surrounding fields they faced almost certain death from Allied field guns, and their prolonged confinement had turned the lanes and tracks into open sewers. The smell of human sweat, horse dung and diesel was inescapable and the eyes of the men were bloodshot from the dust and fumes. All food and horse feed had run out and all that remained were just a few precious litres of water.

Caught in the middle of one of the lanes, General Walther Model waited impatiently in his Mercedes staff car. On his arrival a few days earlier, he had realised that the situation was suicidal and had sent a personal letter to Hitler requesting immediate withdrawal. The returning despatch rider threaded his way towards him. When the reply was finally handed over, Model tore open the envelope and read . . .

"Hold your position."

Within minutes Model heard the faint hum of Typhoons in the distance. As they approached a lane some half a mile away, Model got out of his car and watched as two aircraft broke away from the main formation and climbed almost out of sight. Simultaneously they turned and dived towards opposite ends of the lane. The tiny specks that fell away from them seemed to hang in the air until, on the ground, two bright orange fireballs billowed silently. Huge plumes of black smoke rose up and, after a few seconds, the sound of the explosions reached Model's position.

"*Mein Gott!*" he gasped and raised a pair of binoculars to his eyes.

As the smoke drifted and debris fell back to earth, more Typhoons arrived. Flying fast and low behind one another, pairs of rockets ignited beneath their wings and streaked white vapour towards their targets. Multiple bright yellow and orange explosions mushroomed along the entire length of the lane. One after another the Typhoons raked the lane until it burned like a line of bush fire.

Through his binoculars, Model watched as troops climbed out of blazing tank hatches. Some of them were already on fire while others limped for the cover of the hedgerows. Too far away to hear the screaming, all Model could hear was the distant whine of engines, the crump of explosions and the peaceful breeze in the hedgerow nearby.

After a few minutes, Typhoons turned back towards their bases, but as the sound of their engines faded they were replaced by scores of incoming Spitfires. In tight, low formations they made straight towards the black smoke.

In the operations tent a large map was pinned to a board. From down in the dugout the radio operator relayed information to an Office Sergeant who shaded in sectors within the Nazi enclosure.

"They're on their way back now, sir," said the radio operator.

Bill picked up the field telephone.

"April control to Greycap. You should see the Typhoons above you now."

"Roger," replied Johnnie looking up, "I see them."

"You're clear to make your run. Typhoon leaders report troops hiding in the hedgerows."

Half a mile before he reached the target, Johnnie lined the cross hairs of his sights on a row of Hawthorn trees leading to it. He paused his thumb over the firing button and once next to the line of burning vehicles he pressed it and held it down.

Through his binoculars Model looked on. The wings of each Spitfire sparkled brightly as they took it in turns to empty their magazines along the soft green foliage below.

Back at the Typhoon camp, ground crews worked hard in the midday sun as they hurriedly rearmed and refuelled the hot aircraft. Some pilots stayed sitting in their cockpits eating sandwiches and drinking bottles of water, while some studied maps. Others stood away from their aeroplanes and peed in the grass.

Spent of ammunition, Johnnie's Spitfires withdrew and the

next wave of Typhoons took over.

And so it went on.

After the fifth run of the day, Johnnie eventually led his men back to base in the evening twilight. Behind them, neat rectangles of orange fires and rising palls of black smoke marked the surgical precision of each killing ground. The Spitfires taxied into their maintenance bays and the pilots switched their engines off. Weary ground crews, who had only been able to snatch a few minutes sleep in between raids, went straight to work yet again.

In the airfield dining tent men of all ranks ate together hungrily. The pilots dragged themselves off to bed, while the riggers took deliveries of belts of machine gun and cannon rounds. Out on the airfield, generators hummed and work continued under lamplight. Headlights of fuel trucks going about their rounds, picked out each maintenance bay in turn. Fuel pipes were swung above the wings of the Spitfires, while beneath them riggers reloaded the magazines.

In the briefing tent, tired and unshaven, Johnnie, Dan, Larry and Rafe were briefed by Bill.

"Most of the vehicles have been destroyed within these sectors here. We think Model has given the order to retreat and so you can expect a huge traffic jam through the bottleneck between Faliase here and Arenten here. Any survivors will probably be civilian vehicles heading for the Seine. So look out for any signs of movement. Same goes for the river. And things are getting a little crowded over there, so you may have to stack and queue the American fighters."

With the briefing over, Johnnie finally made his way back to his tent, kicked off his boots, and flopped onto his camp bed.

Before dawn the next day flashes of blue flame dotted around the airfield as the first Spitfire engines were started. In the dormitory tents, pilots awoken abruptly by the noise, heaved themselves out of their beds. Others, more deep in slumber, had to be shaken. In the dining tent pilots ate hastily before making their way out onto the darkness of the airfield.

As Johnnie led his men above the carnage of the previous days attacks, the rising stench of dead bodies was choking. In the distance ahead he spotted a section of American Thunderbolt fighters.

"Greycap to Medicine Man," he coughed, "do you receive? Over."

"Medicine man to Greycap. Copy."

"I think I can see you over sector nine. Can you confirm?"

"You got us, Greycap. We're through over here. But we've still got Eagles over eleven and twelve. Follow me out over ten and look out for bandits in the east."

"Roger Medicine Man. Wilco."

Johnnie's Spitfires followed in an orderly procession behind the Thunderbolts who led him to the River Seine. Below them Seventh Army survivors were spread in a thin line along the bank.

"Greycap to all sections. Larry, Rafe – you wait up here and look out for any bandits. Dan we'll go in first."

Johnnie lined himself up for a low pass along the muddy bank. He chose the crowded river vessels for his first run and, as he took aim, the cross hairs of his sites raced over the water towards them. Six lines of spray kicked up as machine gun and cannon rounds ripped along the river and into the wooden hulls of boats and barges. Amidst the splintered wood flying up, the odd engine boiler blew up billowing grey coal smoke and white steam.

For the rest of the day sector after sector was demolished with industrial repetition. It was a macabre, morbid process which induced a morbid numbness. The contest of guile and airmanship between dog fighting pilots kept nerves and reflexes on the edge. It was not about the man inside the other aeroplane, and the victor felt neither pride nor pity. But the heightened euphoria of staying alive was a sensation like no other. Ground attack was simply a job which had to be done.

By the end of the day the Nazi SS Seventh Army had been completed destroyed and well over ten thousand men and almost as many cart horses lay dead. But that night in the mess tent of the Spitfire camp there was no celebration.

The next day Johnnie and Rafe decided to visit the areas of the attacks and witness the results of their work at first hand. As they approached from several miles away the vile sickly smell of death was so strong Johnnie had to wrap his green silk scarf around his nose and mouth. They passed lane after lane looking for one along which they could drive. But every single one was a solid tangled mass of bodies and burned out tanks and vehicles. Finally they left the jeep and continued on foot until even then it was impossible to walk without the squelch of blood and flesh underfoot. Everywhere was silent but for the buzzing of flies around the bloated corpses which lay rotting in the August sun.

One Mercedes staff car which had careered off the road and

hit a tree caught Rafe's attention, and he walked over for a closer look. He opened the back door expecting to see a dead officer and a driver but to his surprise there was an additional occupant.

"Johnnie! Over here!" he shouted.

Johnnie picked his way over to Rafe.

"In here!" he said.

Johnnie peered into the acrid, hot gloom. In the front, the driver was slumped over the wheel, while in the back a senior army officer had fallen to his knees with his head on the back of the front seat. The duck cloth roof was punctured by several bullet holes and bright spots of sunshine slanted down across the body of a beautiful, well dressed, dark-haired girl in her early twenties. Her silk blouse was soaked in blood but her face was strangely serene.

"My God!" gasped Johnnie.

Chapter Twenty-One
PAY DAY

Following the destruction, the Nazi SS Seventh Army, American, British, Canadian and Free French and Polish ground troops were able to break out of Normandy. Hitler's gamble had failed and the Allies advanced rapidly. In the streets of Paris, General de Gaul led the Free French and the Americans in a liberation parade. The push for the German border was on.

It was supper time in the dining tent at the Normandy Spitfire base, and on the menu there was Bully Beef Stew and bread biscuits – the night before it had been bread biscuits and Bully Beef Stew. Dan, Rafe and Larry stood in the queue with the other pilots as the unappealing slop was ladled onto plates. Johnnie walked in, picked up a plate and joined the queue. An uneasy malaise had set in and for the first time Johnnie witnessed his fun-loving Canadians sitting in gloomy silence. Those that could be bothered just picked at their food.

"Enough!" Johnnie shouted.

Snapped out of their stupor, the startled men looked around at him.

"What we need is a piss up. Come on. We're going out!"

Johnnie walked briskly out of the tent. A dozen puzzled pilots followed him, crammed themselves into a couple of jeeps and they set off in the balmy evening air. After about fifteen minutes or so they eventually found a secluded café in one of the neighbouring villages.

"Okay," said Johnnie, "we don't want to go in mob-handed. So Larry, you come with me and the rest of you wait here. This shouldn't take too long."

Johnnie and Larry climbed out of the jeeps and walked through the entrance and into a cosy, candle-lit atmosphere. The murmur in the room fell silent in an instant and all eyes followed the two men as they squeezed politely past the small round tables. Standing behind the bar, the landlord greeted them cautiously.

"*Qui?*"

"*Bonsoir Monsieur,*" said Johnnie. "*Je suis, erm, nous avez* . . . er . . . Larry?"

Larry introduced himself and in fluent French asked if he and his friends outside could stay for something to eat. The landlord was still uncertain.

"What is this uniform, sir?" he asked. "I do not recognise it."

Feeling somewhat uncomfortable, Larry glanced around to see the disapproving faces amidst the lazy coils of cigarette smoke. Larry whispered back.

"Of course, I'm sorry. This man is a commander in the Royal Air Force and the rest of us are Royal Canadian Air Force. I am French Canadian and we have an American too. We are all pilots."

Breaking into a broad smile the landlord made an excited announcement in French to the rest of his customers.

"British! Canadian! French! American! Why didn't you say? It's alright! These men are our friends. Welcome, welcome!"

The noise of the busy café resumed as quickly as it had stopped as locals stood up, shook hands with the two men and offered them seats at tables. Johnnie made his way back to the door and signalled to the rest of the pilots to come in. The men filed through the front door and were quickly absorbed onto various tables as the landlord brought out red wine and glasses for everyone.

"Gentlemen!" as Larry stood up to speak he hand-gestured for quiet. "Our kind host Marcel, would like to know what you would like to eat. It's on the house!"

The pilots replied almost in chorus.

"Steak. Medium rare!"

A warm, convivial atmosphere grew as the pilots and locals conversed in broken French and English. The landlord's wife and two daughters served up succulent steaks, fresh vegetables and crusty bread and after the meal Cognac, liqueurs and French cigarettes were brought out. As Rafe and Dan attracted the attentions of two pretty local girls, Johnnie caught up on old times with Larry.

"I heard you were shot down over France soon after Bader was captured, but what took you so long to get back?"

"The owner of one of the safe houses had a very pretty daughter!"

"But I always thought you preferred Navy Wrens – black stockings and all that."

"Comme ci, comme ca!" said Larry with a Gallic shrug.

After a while it became clear that Dan and Rafe were becoming too acquainted with the girls for some of the young local men. Johnnie interrupted Larry's own conversation with another girl.

"Larry?" Johnnie nodded in Dan and Rafe's direction. "I

think it might be time to go."

Larry looked over, looked back at Johnnie and then stood up.

"Leave it to me."

As he leaned over the bar, Larry spoke conspiratorially with the landlord. The landlord grinned back and made hand gestures as if giving directions. The local young men conferred with each other, looked back at Dan and Rafe and then stubbed out their cigarettes demonstratively. Larry turned back to Johnnie with a reassuring nod.

"Done!" he said.

Johnnie stood up and addressed the landlord.

"Monsieur, thank you for your kind hospitality, it is much appreciated. But if you will forgive us, we must leave now."

Larry conveyed the gratitude in French and the disappointed pilots reluctantly hauled themselves to their feet and made their way towards the door.

Outside the café Rafe complained to Larry.

"What's going on?" he whinged, "I was just getting lucky, what's the hurry? Why do we have to leave now? I liked that place!"

"Because you're going to like the next place a whole lot more!" said Larry.

The men climbed aboard the jeeps and in the dead of night, Larry navigated along the pitch black country roads until they finally arrived at a large, ornate old building in a small town. The house was in complete darkness. The two jeeps approached slowly and parked a discrete distance away.

Larry jumped out of the jeep and straightened his uniform.

Trying unsuccessfully not to make the metal gate hinges creek, he opened the large metal garden gate and crunched his way along the gravel path. At first he knocked discreetly on the heavy front door but there was no sign of life. He knocked harder and through the crack of one of the wooden bedroom window shutters a dim light appeared and faded again. A minute later the front door opened a little way. Obscured from view of the rest of the men, Giselle, an attractive thirty-year-old held up an oil lamp to see Larry's face and enquire of his business.

"We're pilots Madame. Officers. British, Canadian, French Canadian."

She stepped part way through the door and just into view of the men. Dressed in only a thin negligée, the dim light accentuated her voluptuous hourglass figure. Rafe immediately blew a shrill wolf whistle and Dan clamped his hand over his mouth.

"Quiet! Schmuck!"

Giselle looked over towards the pilots causing a ripple of excitement.

"Are they drunk?" she asked.

"No Madame," said Larry "just very tired. We were wondering if we could come in. We've just been paid. The boys will be no trouble, I promise."

"Who sent you here?"

"Marcel."

"Wait."

Giselle closed the door and dim lights started to appear in the cracks of the window shutters. As Larry walked back to the jeep Dan looked puzzled.

"So what are we going to do," he asked, "take turns?"

The rest of the pilots sniggered loudly.

"Quiet you guys!" demanded Larry, "Come on, fix yourselves up. She's not going to let us in looking like a bunch of slobs!"

The men put on their caps, buttoned up their jackets, straightened their ties and smoothed their uniforms. After about ten minutes the door opened again and Giselle waved them in. Acting sober, the men filed in politely. Inside, the hallway had a huge open sweeping staircase. It was all very elegant, if a little tattered here and there, and from the next room could be heard the light chatter and giggling of feminine voices. Inside the dimly-lit lounge a bevy of pretty, slender girls in their twenties greeted the lovelorn men.

For several weeks the pilots had lived with the smell of cow pat, exhaust fumes and cordite. Now they inhaled au de cologne. They had slept on harsh canvas camp beds and sat in cramped metal cockpits. Now they were offered soft couches and silk cushions. The only clothes they had seen were uniforms, underpants and flying gear. Now they were confronted by stockings, lace and flimsy underwear. They had been kept alive by an energy-sapping mixture of adrenaline, testosterone and amphetamine. Now they were no longer on the edge and could relax. The only people they had seen were each other, gnarled and battle-weary, grubby and unshaven. Now they gazed upon luxurious long hair, soft curves and smooth skin.

"Please, sit down," said Giselle and she beckoned the men towards the girls who welcomed them.

"*Bonsoir* . . . welcome . . . wine?"

Before everyone got to know one another too well, Giselle conferred discretely with Larry in French.

"My girls are all very beautiful, are they not?"

"Yes. Yes of course, Madame. Without a doubt."

"And your men would like to stay the night, yes?"

"Yes, that was kind of the idea?"

Then with a tactful business-like smile Giselle listed her fees.

"In advance, if you please?"

"Yes, yes of course!"

Larry went around to each pilot in turn and they emptied their pockets of cash. Not knowing quite what to do, Johnnie sat down on a chaise longue while Giselle took the money into a back room and locked it in a strong box. When she returned she cranked the gramophone and played a crackly French recording of *Lily Marleen*.

"*Devant la caserne, quand le jour s'en fuit . . .*"

Starved of female comfort, the men wasted no time in becoming entwined with their hosts. Two of the girls had made a beeline for Rafe who basked in the attention.

"Look at your beautiful blond hair! . . . So handsome, yet so young!"

"Well, that's really nice of you, but I'm sorry I can't afford to pay twice."

The girls just smiled and draped themselves around him.

Johnnie grinned with satisfaction at his boys at play. But much to the amusement of Dan and Larry, when Giselle sat next to him he kept a straight-backed, respectful distance.

Carefree cavorting eventually became more carnal and, driven by urgent desire, the men were led out of the lounge and up the stairway. One of the last to leave the room was Dan, but before making his way towards the door he checked in Johnnie's direction only to see that the chaise longue was already empty.

Chapter Twenty-Two
RUDE AWAKENING

It was daybreak at Kenway and Clarke stood looking over the shoulder of the radar operator. One by one, tiny white spots started to appear on the screen.

"Now, what are they up to?" he said to himself.

He walked over to the controller's seat and looked down over the plotting table. WAAFs placed numerous Swastika markers over Paris. The nearest RAF wing to them was indicated with a marker bearing the initials 'AC'. Clarke picked up the telephone receiver and pressed the scrambler button.

"April Control? Morning Bill. We've got some trade for you over the River Seine ... "

At the Spitfire camp, Bill McCord stood in front of the map in the operations tent and repeated the coordinates phoned through to him by Clarke, while the Operations Sergeant marked them on the map. At the same time the radio operator repeated the coordinates of similar sightings from ground spotters. He wrote the numbers down on a piece of paper and handed up from the dugout to Bill who nodded back.

"East of the River Seine ... yes ... yes ... 109s most likely and maybe some 190s. Yes, we have confirmation. They're probably covering the last of the stragglers from the Falaise area."

In the bedrooms of Giselle's house the comatose pilots slept off the previous night's excesses. Outside two RAF military policemen parked next to the pilot's jeeps. They stepped out of the car, looked over the outside of the building and then rapped hard on the door. Startled by the sudden racket, Giselle got up out of bed, pushed her hair out of her groggy eyes and wrapped her negligée around herself. As she made her way down the stairs the military policeman continued to hammer on the door.

"Military police. Open up!" the Sergeant bellowed.

"*Mon dieu!*"

She unlocked the door and squinted in the painful morning sunlight at the two enormous, red-capped MPs who looked down at her. Bolt upright and with a swagger stick under his arm, the stern Sergeant MP caught a glimpse of her cavernous cleavage and allowed himself an admiring grin.

"Sorry Luv, but we need to come in."

Giselle opened the door and the two men walked straight past her and up the stairs.

"Come along gentlemen!" they shouted. "We leave in five minutes . . . everyone on your feet please . . . come along . . . wake up . . . briefing in thirty minutes!"

Tired, and very hung over, the pilots staggered out of the bedrooms pulling up their trousers and tucking in their shirts. Rafe was followed out onto the landing by his two girls and he turned for parting kisses.

The night before, the roads had seemed smooth enough but on the way back to the Spitfire camp they were hideously bumpy and thudded repeatedly inside sore heads. Those who felt worse for wear tried to avoid each other as they threw up over the sides of the jeeps. Rafe couldn't decide which of his problems was more urgent and when they reached the airfield he dashed straight into the latrines. Outside, the rest of the pilots could hear him throwing up, and farting.

"Oh God!" he groaned.

Johnnie, Larry and Dan collected their flying gear from their tents and were met by Bill who briefed them as they walked hurriedly towards their Spitfires.

"One nineties," said Bill, "east of the Seine."

"Height?" asked Johnnie burping, "number?"

"About fifty or so – Clarke's still working on it. He'll brief you once you're over Paris. But we think there are two groups of them."

As Rafe caught them up he pulled on his flying gear and wiped his mouth.

"Okay," said Johnnie. "Dan, you come with me and we'll go west. Larry, Rafe you keep below us on our port and guard east – and Larry, listen out for any French RT."

The pilots climbed into their cockpits, held their masks to their faces and sucked in hard at the oxygen to try and clear their hangovers. The coordinates were handed to Johnnie and he checked them against his map before quickly running through the start-up procedure.

Within minutes the pilots took off in sections of four and the entire wing assembled in tight V-formations. Once they were over the River Seine Clarke radioed from Kenway.

"Two sections of twenty, plus one high. one low. Two miles, ten degrees port."

"Roger, Grass Seed. Greycap to wing. Split now but maintain

the same height."

As the wing turned in a wide arc to port, it divided smoothly into two squadrons each with three sections of V-formations of four. Larry and Rafe flew the east of the River while Johnnie and Dan flew the west. Then they spotted two large unidentified sections of fighters.

"Can you tell what they are, Dan?" asked Johnnie.

"Can't make them out, Johnnie. Could be Americans."

"Dan, we'll check above the high section of bandits. Larry, Rafe you stay and cover the low section. Let me know if you can identify them."

Johnnie and Dan led their sections, climbed steep and turned hard to the west. From upside down Johnnie looked through the top of his canopy.

"They're bandits alright!" he said. "One nineties! Can you see their markings?"

"Roger," replied Dan, "they're Huns. 190s above, 109s below."

"Dan, we'll take the top bunch. Larry, Rafe – you take the section below. We've got the sun behind us so they can't see us. Everyone move in and wait for my call."

Keeping in strict V-formations of four, the two separate squadrons of Spitfires each turned above and behind the two groups of enemy fighters.

"Attack formations," said Johnnie.

Every section of four Spitfires fanned out into the well-rehearsed attacking claw. As Johnnie moved into position the sun shone from above and behind him illuminating his instruments and highlighting the enemy fighters below.

"Wait . . .wait," he said calmly. The pilots flicked their safety catches to 'armed' and waited, but some of them were not correctly in position. The element of surprise would be lost in a badly coordinated strike and allow the enemy the chance of a costly counter attack. As vital seconds ticked by Johnnie made his final preparation.

"Rafe, two of your sections are about to undershoot. Pull them in tighter and aim them higher."

"Roger, Greycap," said Rafe and he ordered his men into position.

"Everyone get in – now!" called Johnnie.

In two mass simultaneous attacks, the Spitfires sliced down through the enemy formations with surgical precision, each firing on a different target.

In the upper attack, six 190s were shot down in rapid succession. Two exploded and the rest spiralled down in smoke. Johnnie raked his target, and as it turned on its back he hit the fuel tank and it burst into a ball of flame.

In the lower attack five 109s were shot down at the same time. Once beneath the two enemy formations, Johnnie radioed again.

"Looks like these buggers want to make a fight of it. Everyone turn back in!"

All the Spitfires turned back towards them and as individual dog fights broke out all around, the sky was filled with twirling aircraft as opposing pilots tried to turn behind one another.

Johnnie found a stray 190 and was just about to fire on it when he saw the Ace of Clubs closing on the tail of Rafe. He broke off his attack, flew away from the swarm and directly towards his old adversary.

"Rafe," he called urgently, "on your tail!"

Johnnie was unable to line up his sights, but his burst of fire was enough to drive the Ace of Clubs away and into the sun. Johnnie squinted in the glare and swivelled his head all around in search of his target but he had already lost him. And suddenly he was alone.

Disorientated and momentarily blinded by the sun, Johnnie looked up at the mirror above his cockpit to see the Ace of Clubs side-slipping silently into view. Instinctively, he turned hard and fast left and right. His mouth became dry and his legs trembled. He tried a barrel roll and inverted dive but he couldn't shake off his attacker.

On the ground the Allies were still shelling the SS troops on the west bank of the River Seine and Johnnie made for the rising columns of black smoke. Again and again he turned in between them but still he could not lose his predator. The same sickening fear of Dieppe two years earlier returned to clench his stomach.

Above the rooftops of Paris, Johnnie took a gamble on power. He pulled the stick back hard and pushed the throttle to maximum. The Ace of Clubs fired as he tried to climb with him but the Merlin 61 delivered and in a hail of tracer Johnnie surged high above in an upward roll. Having gained the advantage of height Johnnie seized his opportunity, half rolled into a dive and spotted the Focke Wulf's familiar ace of clubs marking below the cockpit. His mouth was no longer dry, his legs stopped shaking and his stomach untwisted. For the first time ever he had taken control over his tormentor.

Calmness flowed through him as if back on the fields of Leicestershire. Just feet above the River Seine Johnnie gave chase upstream. Fleeting chances of a shot flicked back and forth across his sights but he knew he only had a few seconds of ammunition left. The shot would have to be perfect.

In search of cover the Ace of Clubs made an unexpected left turn up a narrow tributary. On both sides of the water the branches of dense trees hung over and nearly touched in parts. As his quarry dived beneath them Johnnie's view became obscured by a storm of leaves swirling from its wing tips. To avoid the deadly turbulence, Johnnie flew above and waited for his target to re-emerge.

An uncomfortable sense of danger made Johnnie look up. Ahead, in a clearing between the trees, he saw power cables hanging low over the water. His crafty opponent was leading him directly into a trap. With no time to climb above the cables he was forced down and was immediately thrown around in the Ace of Clubs's slipstream. As he wrestled hard with stick and rudder, he struggled to avoid hitting the cables or ditching into the river, and the turbulence nearly flicked him into a spin. With only feet of clearance above and below a split second slip of hand or foot would result in certain death.

As the Ace of Clubs slowed down to a casual climb, Johnnie saw the pilot looking back down at him. With a nonchalant wave Johnnie was bade farewell by the man who waited for the spectacle of his fatal crash. Even as the controls thrashed chaotically at his hands and feet, Johnnie raged at the smug assumption. His Spitfire dipped violently and the ripples on the surface of the murky green water reared up at him.

With one last pull on the stick and pushing the throttle into maximum, Johnnie cleared the water with inches to spare and entered smooth, calm air. The shudder from the controls was resumed to fluid and harmonious responsiveness as the cross hairs of his sights swung towards the startled spectator. In a frantic bid to escape, the Ace of Clubs pulled up in a hard and tight left-turning climb. With blood draining from his head, Johnnie's vision greyed out as he pulled his Spitfire to the edge in the tightest turn he could.

But with his magazine low there would only be enough for a five second burst, maybe less. No time for calculations. The instinct of the country boy took over and Johnnie lost sight of the target as he aimed the nose of his Spitfire high and wide. With his thumb paused over the firing button he kept turning until the angle felt right. The shot was on.

Machine gun rounds and cannon shells flashed from the Spitfire's wings but after three seconds the noisy chatter ran into an empty 'click, click, click'.

Tracer arced smoothly over the tree tops and found the engine of the Ace of Clubs, ripping down the middle of its length to the tail. White glycol vapour poured from the cowling, followed by black smoke and bright flame. For a few moments the stricken aircraft righted itself into level flight and began to glide. There was no parachute but there was still just enough time for Johnnie's adversary to bale out. Then to his disbelief, and with seemingly unfeasible control, the Ace of Clubs was brought down in a smooth emergency landing approach. But with the flames spreading at fifty feet it dived steeply. In one final act of defiance the nose was pulled and it belly landed on the ground, bounced up and exploded into a copse of trees.

One man had died and one had survived. Had they met under different circumstances they might even have had a drink together.

But there was no time for reflection. Realising the crash would draw the attention of any other enemy fighters in the area, Johnnie went in search of a friendly formation.

"Greycap to Larry. I'm just east of the Seine. Where are you?"

"Larry to Greycap. In the same area above you at fifteen thousand. Where the hell have you been? Are you alright?"

"*Comme ci, comme ca*. Any sign of the rest of them?"

"No. We've had a bit of a ding dong up here, but now they've cleared off. Shall we come down?"

"No, stay there. I'll climb up to you."

As Johnnie climbed up in a wide, spiralling turn he spotted the canopies of six fighters glinting in the sun.

"Greycap to Larry. I see you now. I'll rock my wings and you can form up behind me."

As he flew into the lead position and rocked his wings, orange tracer suddenly flashed over the top of his canopy. He broke hard right and looked back to see six Messerschmitts moving in to surround him. The lead pilot fired again.

"Christ!"

Johnnie barrel rolled over and turned into a tight right-hand climb but the Me 109s stayed with him. Two moved onto his starboard wing, two onto his port and two stayed behind. Taking it in turns, the outermost enemy fighters tried to turn in on him but they were unable to turn tight enough. Johnnie's vision turned to grey and a black circle bounded his peripheral vision. He opened the oxygen bottle to full and gulped hard. The altimeter wound up steadily to 16,000 feet as the dark circle became smaller. At 16,500 feet another 109 attacked and the Spitfire shuddered as a cannon shell punched through its starboard wing root.

Again and again the 109s swooped and Johnnie pulled still harder on the stick. Tracer flew all around him and his peripheral vision shrank on the altimeter as it passed over 17,000 feet. The strength began to drain from his arms and at 18,500 feet his head flopped sideways, his hearing faded and the altimeter disappeared in the black.

Nineteen thousand feet. THUMP! The loud Supercharger kicked in with a huge jolt and Johnnie's Spitfire was thrown forward in a massive surge of acceleration. Pinned back in his seat he straightened out of the turn and blinked hard. As his eyesight and hearing restored he checked the rear view mirror to see the Messerschmitts falling uselessly behind. Then he checked the fuel gauge.

EMPTY!

Chapter Twenty-Three
MORTALITY

With his Spitfire hit for the first time, all of his ammunition spent and his fuel about to run out, Johnnie's return to camp was low, slow and very cautious. If he spotted any enemy aircraft his only chance would be to make a forced landing and run for cover. With every field that he passed he eyed up potential sites.

Eventually the Spitfire camp came into view but when he was at fifty feet on his final approach, the engine cut out. Painful memories of his training days at Hawarden flashed through his mind, but this time he glided down in a perfect emergency landing and a fuel truck drove over to meet him.

Once back in his maintenance bay his ground crew helped him to unfasten his harness and he climbed out of the cockpit to inspect the damage. The engine made tinkling noises of cooling as he walked round to the starboard wing. The exit hole from the cannon shell was circled by torn-up aluminium like sunflower leaves. If it had passed just a few inches further to the left it would have shot straight through the fuel tank and the cockpit seat above it.

Johnnie took out his cigarettes from his breast pocket, but his hands shook so badly that he was unable to strike a match. One of the riggers lit up one of his own cigarettes and passed it to him.

"Thanks," he said appreciatively and with a leery glance at the hole he apologised.

"Sorry about that. Bit crowded up there."

As he took a long, calming drag from his cigarette, Dan walked up to him with a note in his hand and a fearful look on his face.

"What?" asked Johnnie. "WHAT!"

"It's Paula," said Dan handing over the note, "she's had a boy but there were complications. She's in a bad way, Johnnie."

"How bad?"

"We don't know. All we have been told is that you have got to go back there as soon as possible."

"But that won't be for another week!"

"Bill has said he will come back in a couple of days and cover for you."

In the mess tent that evening the usual rowdy drinking games were in full swing. Outside, away from the noise, Johnnie sat on a stack of wooden supply boxes and smoked as he gazed trance-like at the stars. In a hospital on the other side of the English Channel he had a son. Was he alright? And what of Paula, was she alive? Within forty-eight hours he would know. They were to be the longest forty-eight hours he would ever know.

Over the airfield at the Tangmere, Johnnie circled as the early morning mist lifted. With the canopy locked open he throttled back, gently bleeding the airspeed away with the height, as he brought the Spitfire down into the crosswind.

UNDERCARRIAGE	DOWN
AIRSPEED	140 MPH

FLAPS	DOWN
HEIGHT	250 FT

He side-slipped down into the final approach and then straightened up and trickled back the power. Sinking, sinking, sinking – then he felt the first bounce on the main wheels, the bump from the tail wheel and the rumble across the airfield towards the awaiting riggers.

With the engine cut the whirring gyros wound down behind the instrument panel, and the faint smell of petrol, glycol and oil seeped up.

MAGNETO SWITCHES	OFF
FUELCOCK LEVERS	OFF
RADIO	OFF
OXYGEN	OFF AND DISCONNECT

It was all an automatic routine. Johnnie climbed out of the cockpit and gave a nod of thanks to the riggers. Where had he just come from? "Oh yes, France. That's right." In the car park outside the officer's mess his Lagonda was waiting and, without stopping for breakfast, he set off for Norfolk. As he drove through the villages of Sussex he saw billboards outside newsagents declaring: 'Paris Liberated' and 'Allies march on Germany'.

Outside the hospital the car park was quiet. Tired and gaunt from two sleepless nights, Johnnie stepped out of the car and straightened his uniform. Whatever news awaited him, within the next few minutes he would find out. At first he did not want to move. Standing in the car park there was no pain, only uncertainty. But then he braced himself for the worst and walked briskly up to the main entrance. Inside the building he removed his cap, tucked it under his arm and made his enquiry at the reception desk.

"Morning Wing Commander," said the Matron. "How can I help you?"

"It's my wife, Pauline. Pauline Johnson."

The Matron's disposition suddenly became more serious and called to a nurse who was passing by carrying an armful of files.

"Yes, right. Nurse! Mrs. Johnson. Would you show the Wing Commander the way?"

"Certainly," said the nurse, "this way please."

Johnnie walked with the nurse along the corridor, too slowly for his liking.

Show him where? Show him somewhere – she must be alive. The nurse's crisp, starched, blue uniform rustled against the clicking of their footsteps on the hard linoleum floor. Disinfectant curdled with the smell of polishing wax. On a distant ward the faint sound of a radio could be heard. The Andrews Sisters sang *Boogie Woogie Company Boy*, in cheerful contradiction to his anticipation. At the end of the corridor the nurse turned and led him up the stone steps. He could not wait any longer.

"How . . . er . . . how is she?" he asked trying to remain calm, "And the baby?"

"The baby's fine," said the nurse, "but your wife has had a very tough time of it. She's lost a lot of blood and she's very weak."

"But, she will be okay?"

"The doctors seem to think so. She's not stopped asking about you – but try to keep this brief, she needs the rest."

When they reached Paula's room the nurse stopped.

"In here. I'll come back in ten minutes."

Through the frosted glass of the door, the room was dimmed by partially drawn curtains. A slot of daylight shone on the foot of the bed and Johnnie could just make out Paula's dark hair against the white pillow. He turned the handle, stepped quietly into the room and clicked the door closed behind him. There was a cot next to the far side of the bed but the baby was hidden by its high sides. A baby! Not just Paula there was another person in the room. But for her shallow breathing Paula lay motionless and her face was pale.

Johnnie stepped forward, put his cap on the bed and kneeled by the side of it. At first he just stared. Then he held Paula's hand, moved his face near to hers and whispered.

"Paula . . . Paula."

Paula's eyes opened and she slowly rocked her head to look at Johnnie.

"Johnnie!" she whispered, barely audible. "I thought you were, that you . . ."

"I'm here darling."

The baby made a gurgling noise and Johnnie looked over at the cot. Paula smiled weakly.

"Say hello to your son."

Johnnie rose quietly to his feet, walked around the bed and looked into the cot at the tiny boy who was just stirring from his sleep.

With one big hand cupped under his body and one under his head, he gently lifted him up. He could feel the little movements of the soft, warm bundle. When he held the baby's face against his, he could feel his tiny breaths against his cheek. His eyes filled with tears and his throat tightened.

"Oh! – My boy!"

Chapter Twenty-Four
FINAL CROSSING

14 April 1945, Friedrichroda, Germany

In the hill forests, 160 km north east of Frankfurt, a small American armoured column made its way along a dirt track. In the lead staff car, Colonel Boardman of the US Third Army was accompanied by Scrine. Following behind them was an armoured car and a truck carrying troops. Scrine checked the coordinates on the map and looked around. Then he spotted a small concealed warehouse and pointed to it. The column stopped a safe distance away and the armoured car drove to the front of the column. The troops jumped down from the truck and the sergeant ordered them to surround the warehouse. The troops cocked their rifles and nervously crept into position. With their backs to the warehouse they checked all around for signs of the enemy.

The sergeant waved the 'all clear' to Boardman and he and Scrine approached, flanked by a guard of four GIs. The large, sliding doors of the warehouse were padlocked and so a hefty pair of chain cutters had to be used to free them. Two GIs slid the doors open and peered in as a bright slot of light penetrated the darkness. One GI knelt down on one knee while the other stood above him. With machine guns to their shoulders they held flashlights next to them as they surveyed the interior of the warehouse.

Then one flashlight fell on the stubby nose of a large, dark, motionless figure. Like the eyes of a huge, menacing, flying monster, at each side of the nose was a round, jet engine air intake. At first the GIs were startled and nearly opened fire, but as they swung their flashlights around they followed the graceful wings of the aircraft's unusual form.

"Je-sus!" said one of the GIs.

The doors were opened wider and six more GIs entered the warehouse followed by Boardman, Scrine and a military photographer. As their eyes adjusted to the darkness they surrounded their discovery and its eerie outline became clear.

"That it?" asked Boardman.

"That's it!" said Scrine.

With the doors fully opened the mysterious aircraft stood in broad daylight. It looked just like a giant bat. It had no tail, no rudder, no fuselage and no propeller. Just a simple jet-propelled flying wing. It was a creation of such unearthly futuristic design that the Colonel had to touch it as if to check it was real. The military photographer clicked busily from different angles.

"Lieutenant!" shouted Boardman. "Take the film out of that camera and destroy it. No one is to say a word to anyone about this. Is that clear?"

May 1945, Brussels

Towards the end of the Allied advance towards Germany, Johnnie had been promoted to Group Captain and had settled his men in the officer's mess of a former Nazi airbase. After living under canvas for so long their new accommodation was more than welcome.

Since the previous September, Hitler had commenced his V2 rocket offensive against London, but as the Allied ground troops pushed the Nazi's out of Holland, they had to be launched from further away and could only reach as far as East Anglia. With the Allied High Command still unsure of what Hitler might be hiding, the search for his weapons of mass destruction would not be over until Germany had been searched thoroughly.

With the final push for Berlin underway, it was only a matter of time before Allied troops on the west would make contact with Russian forces in the east. Not surprisingly, word soon reached Johnnie of yet another move and, as he packed his belongings in readiness, Bill McCord called by. Sitting by Johnnie's desk Bill looked out of the window at pilots and ground crews who were making their final preparations.

"So Johnnie, now that you've broken Sailor Malan's record, what's next?"

"An end to this war."

"You know you only need two more kills and your score will pass forty. That's some achievement."

"Thanks Bill," answered Johnnie without looking up.

"Well," Bill persisted, "do you think you can break forty?"

"I don't know Bill. I can't tell you."

"Are you going to try?"

Johnnie straightened up, looked through the window at the pilots outside and spoke with weary reflection.

"You know – when Bader went missing none of us knew what to do next. Then we carried on where he left off. Back then it was our turn," Johnnie nodded in the direction of the pilots outside, "now it's theirs."

"But if you do it Johnnie, it will be another record – and great reading for the folks back home."

Suddenly, in the distance, the incandescent glow of a V2 rocket taking off was seen climbing high into the sky. Johnnie and Harry looked with grim alarm. A spiral vapour trail traced its deadly path and the delayed thunder clap of the breaking sound barrier was heard.

"Berlin can't wait for records to be broken Bill. Let's just finish this thing and go home."

Following a report by ground troops of Nazi fighter activity over Berlin, Johnnie led a search patrol of four Spitfires. It had been nearly six years since he had first worn the uniform of a Sergeant Pilot and nearly one thousand missions later, Group Captain Johnson was still on the lookout for the enemy. But now all it would take would be one stray cannon shell and a family at home would be left without a father. As always Johnnie went about his fighting with workmanlike caution and method.

"Greycap to Greycap section. Bandits. Four of them, ten o'clock high one mile."

"Roger, Greycap. I have them," Dan replied.

"Orbit here," said Johnnie calmly, "I'll call the break."

Johnnie's section kept a strict V-formation as it flew in a wide circle.

"They're coming down, Johnnie," said Larry.

"Keep turning, nobody break," ordered Johnnie. "Keep turning."

He squinted up at the Fock Wulf leader. After a few tense

moments the Nazi pilot waggled his wings and lowered his wheels.

"That's it!" said Johnnie. "It's over. Let's take them back. Form up around them."

Dan moved to the starboard of the Nazi fighters, Larry to port and Rafe to the rear as Johnnie led his captives back to base.

The following morning he awoke at dawn as usual. He checked his watch and listened, silence. For the first time in his six years with the RAF he was not being disturbed by the sound of early morning engine checks. He swung his legs out of bed, walked over to the window and pulled back the curtains. Two rows of Spitfires stood unattended with their canopy covers on and wheel chocks in place. He looked around the airfield. Not a soul in sight.

All over Europe and North America people packed into the squares of cities and partied around the clock. Service men and women hugged and kissed with civilians in celebration and relief.

On Welbeck estate, the Duke of Portland held champagne celebrations with shooting guests. In Staveley, miner's families held street parties with newspaper party hats and meagre rations. In the aircraft factories around the UK workers danced the conga on the shop floors. On the workshop floor of the Spitfire factory in Castle Bromwich, Stanley Woodley and Geoff Hives brought in crates of beer for the workers.

June 1945, Norwich
Johnnie parked his Lagonda outside a small terraced cottage.

Inside Paula had not been expecting him home for another week. She opened the front door and, breathless with surprise, she immediately threw her arms around his neck and held on to him tight. She laughed and cried at the same time and for a few moments they just stayed there not moving or saying anything. The dread of the knock on the door from the postman delivering the 'killed in action' telegram would never happen. The pain of uncertainty was over. He was home.

On the middle of the living room floor, his nine-month old son sat in his cot. The last time Johnnie had seen him there was no eye contact and no facial expression, just a gurgling newborn with fidgeting arms and legs.

Johnnie put his cap on the armchair and kneeled down beside the cot and just looked. No more going away for a good while now. For the time being he would have his family to himself. Gently he picked the little boy up, lifted him high above his head and laughed out loud with joy.

"We had a long love affair, you and I. You, the most beautiful fighter ever built, and me the happy proud pilot. We grew up together in combat over England and Europe. And when it was over we crossed the Channel together for the last time, as we had done a thousand times before. The contrails that marked the air battles have long been swept away and the grass is long on some of the graves of those who fell. But as long as men fly – you, my beautiful Spitfire, will be remembered." *

'Johnnie' Johnson.

*Extract taken from *The Great Adventure* by James Edgar 'Johnnie' Johnson.

© Copyright Christopher Johnson

EPILOGUE

The 'batwing' aircraft discovered by the US Third Army at Friedrichroda turned out to be the Horten 229, which was the world's first jet-powered Stealth Fighter. In 1945 Walter and Reimar Horten were working on a long-range Stealth Bomber, the Horten 18.

Some historians argue that if World War Two in Europe had lasted into 1946, Hitler would have possessed weapons which could have changed its outcome. He might even have had the capability of dropping nuclear bombs on American cities.

During World War Two, 'Johnnie' Johnson shot down a total of thirty-eight enemy aircraft which was the highest score of any Allied fighter pilot in Europe during that conflict. He was the REAL top gun and possibly the greatest Spitfire leader of all time.

As one of the most highly decorated RAF pilots in history he was feted by royalty, but he never lost the common touch and celebrated with friends of all ranks in ordinary pubs.

Loughborough Grammar School included Johnnie in their Alumni and he became one of its most honoured beneficiaries. In July 1957 he arrived by helicopter to open one of the biggest fund-raising events in the school's history.

In 1969 he retired from the RAF at the rank of Air Vice-Marshall but memory of those made homeless during the Blitz stayed with him. During the same year he founded the Johnnie Johnson Housing Trust, a non-profit organisation which, at the time of writing, provides five thousand homes for the vulnerable and the disadvantaged.

He was never knighted.

'Johnnie' Johnson by Cuthbert Orde, 1943

Air Vice-Marshall
James Edgar Johnson
CB, CBE, DSO & Two Bars, DFC & Bar
9 March 1915 – 30 January 2001

ACKNOWLEDGEMENTS

First and most importantly I must thank the Johnson family for their time, generosity and hospitality. In particular Johnnie's younger son Chris has been most helpful in loaning me an extensive collection of unique archive material. He also arranged a meeting where we recorded an interview with Johnnie's younger brother, Ross.

I would also like to thank all of the following people:

Jim Lunney and Des Oxley of the Johnnie Johnson Housing Trust, Stockport, for providing information on what it was like to work with Johnnie.

The Headmaster of Loughborough Grammar School, Mr. P. B. Fisher and the Deputy Headmaster Mr. John Weitzel, for their time during my visit there and for allowing me access to school archive material.

The Historian and Librarian, Tony Sharkey, of Blackpool Central Library, for providing biographic detail on the comedian, Dave Morris.

Glen Jackson, president and historian of Blackpool North Shore Golf Club, for his time during my visit there, and for providing me with details of Blackpool's war-time history.

Finally, special thanks to my friend and advisor Barrie Penty, for his patience and invaluable critique throughout the entire project.

REFERENCES

Archive materials:
By Kind permission of Christopher Johnson: Various archive materials known collectively as *The Johnson Papers* including:

Photo copies of RAF log books of J. E. Johnson 1939–1945
Personal diary of J. E. Johnson 1942
Copies of World War photographs of J. E. Johnson with an index
Copies of personal articles on and eulogies of J. E. Johnson
World War Two RAF annual confidential course reports for J. E. Johnson
Personal combat report for J. E. Johnson
Script and video of *This is your Life,* 1985 (Thames Television)
Newspaper cuttings from *The Daily Sketch* 1939–45
Newspaper cuttings from *The Daily Express* 1956

Personal interview with Johnnie's younger brother, Ross: Recorded in Oakham, Rutland, UK. 23 November 2012

By kind permission of the Headmaster Mr. P. B. Fisher and the Deputy Headmaster John Weitzel of Loughborough Grammar School:

The Loughburian 1931, 32 & 33
Loughborough Monitor 13 December 1945

The Echo (Loughborough) 14 December 1945
Loughborough Grammar School Fete (programme) 20 July
    1957

Videos:

'Hitler's Stealth Jet Fighter' *National Geographic* Military
    Documentary
'Spitfire!' Documentary, with Raymond Baxter. BBC Two 1976
"R. J. Mitchell – The Spitfire Documentary" Inca Productions.

Internet:

Spartacus Educational www.spartacus.schoolnet.co.uk

Books:

Wing Leader, J. E. Johnson 1956 Random House Publishing
Spitfire Ace of Aces, Dilip Sarkar2011 Amberley Publishing
Johnnie Johnson: Spitfire Top Gun, Part One, Dilip Sarkar 2002
    Ramrod Publications
Johnnie Johnson: Spitfire Top Gun, Part Two, Dilip Sarkar 2005
    Victory Publications
The Great Adventure, J. E. Johnson © Copyright Christopher
    Johnson
One Hundred Years of Golf Around The Knowle, produced
    by Blackpool, North Shore Golf Club.

Newspaper obituaries:

Daily Telegraph 1 February 2001
The Guardian 1 February 2001
New York Times 1 February 2001